HoneyKeep Minist

eyKeep Ministries

HoneyKeep Minist

neyKeep Ministries

HoneyKeep Minist

eyKeep Ministries

THE PROMISELAND ADVENTURES . . . .

Rufus and Clyde and The STENCH OF DOOM Mini

2nd Edition

Written, Edited and Illustrated by Cheryl Jones
(2017 8.5x11 print publication) 978-0-9989332-0-7
Proofread by Cheryl Wagner
(2017 8.5x11 print publication) 978-0-9989332-0-7
Revised by Cheryl Jones (2019 6x9 print publication) 978-0-9989332-3-8
Proofread by Cheryl Jones (2019 6x9 print publication) 978-0-9989332-3-8

HoneyKeep Ministries

170 Manhattan Street #174
Buffalo NY, 14215

"Keeping the sweetness of Jesus in your heart everyday"

ISBN-13: 978-0-9989332-3-8
ISBN-10: 0-9989332-3-6

Reach us by phone or online
716-235-4575
www.honeykeepministries.org

About the founder:

Cheryl Jones love for art, crafts and writing started as a child. Born and raised in Buffalo NY, her family was a constant encourager for pursuing her artistic endeavors. That influence only deepened as she discovered Christ. Her love for watching and creating cartoons with an interesting story line grew stronger with each passing year. In 2015; she felt the call of starting her own publishing company called HoneyKeep Ministries.

Her goal through HoneyKeep Ministries is to provide daily devotions of God's word with a touch of humor and inspiration. This ministry is all about encouragement and staying strong within the faith on a daily basis, something that kids, adults who are children-at-heart (like herself!!) and families can enjoy together.

IMPORTANT MESSAGE FROM MANAGEMENT:

We at HoneyKeep Ministries want to thank each of our many fans for their support of our ministry. We are still in our infant stages and apologize for any imperfections (grammar issues) that may be discovered while reading our material. We pray that you will be patient with us and we strongly encourage you to contact us and make us aware of whatever you may discover. We also encourage our customers to contact us with feedback on how our ministry has touched you and what it has done for you overall. Our contact information is listed below:

HoneyKeep Ministries Publications

170 Manhattan Street #174

Buffalo NY, 14215

716-235-4575

www.honeykeepministries.org

And a special Thanks to Auntie Shirley, Mrs. Cheryl, Cousin Keshia, my Mom and so many more for believing that this dream of mine could really come true. Love you guys! And to my son, little David, mommy loves you very much!!

HoneyKeep Ministries

Table of Contents

Instructions for Devotional

HEY KIDS, welcome to the wacky world of Manna's Ville!

Each fun filled day offers bits and pieces of a story that you follow for 90 days. In addition; you will be given a daily bible scripture and activity to do. You can use the *"90 Day Bible Scripture List"* for the entire 3 months to read the scripture of the day. And here's the instructions for the additional activities:

Fill In the Missing Words: Use the *"90 Day Bible Scriptures List"* and fill in the missing words from the scriptures.

Word Search: Find the words listed (answers located in the back of the book).

Circle All/ Cross Out List: Circle or cross out all that applies and also use the *"Books of Bible List"* for assistance when needed (answers located in the back of the book).

Seeking God Page: Color the black and white picture.

Connect the Matching things: Draw a line connecting the matching things (answers located in the back of the book).

My To Do List/ My Daily Planner: Write down your goals for the day.

Means To Me: Express whatever the list of three things means to you.

My Special Prayer: Write down your special prayer from the heart to God.

Answer the 4 Questions: Answer the multiple choice questions, True/False questions, Yes/No questions to the best of your ability (answers located in the back of the book).

Draw Your Masterpiece/Sketch Time/Draw a Picture: Draw the featured picture of the day to the best of your ability.

Reading Olympic Challenge: Try to read the featured story as instructed to the best of your ability.

Play Cards: Play Memory Card Game with card cut outs.

Books of the Bible

OLD TESTAMENT

Genesis
Exodus
Leviticus
Numbers
Deuteronomy
Joshua
Judges
Ruth
1 Samuel
2 Samuel
1 Kings
2 Kings
1 Chronicles
2 Chronicles
Ezra
Nehemiah
Esther
Job
Psalms
Proverbs

Ecclesiastes
Song of Solo-
mon
Isaiah
Jeremiah
Lamentations
Ezekiel
Daniel
Hosea
Joel
Amos
Obadiah
Jonah
Micah
Nahum
Habakkuk
Zephaniah
Haggai
Zechariah
Malachi

NEW TESTAMENT

Matthew
Mark
Luke
John
Acts
Romans
1 Corinthians
2 Corinthians
Galatians
Ephesians
Philippians
Colossians
1 Thessalonians
2 Thessalonians

1 Timothy
2 Timothy
Titus
Philemon
Hebrews
James
1 Peter
2 Peter
1 John
2 John
3 John
Jude
Revelation

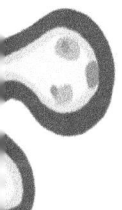

90 Day Bible Scriptures (Day 1 thru Day 17)

(Hosea 10: 12) "Sow to yourselves in righteousness, reap in mercy; break up your fallow ground: for it is time to seek the Lord, till he come and rain righteousness upon you" Day 1

(1 Chronicles 28:9) "And thou, Solomon my son, know thou the God of thy father, and serve him with a perfect heart and with a willing mind: for the Lord searcheth all the hearts, and understandeth all the imaginations of the thoughts: if thou seek him, he will be found of thee; but if thou forsake him, he will cast thee off for ever" Day 2

(2 Chronicles 15:2) "And he went out to meet Asa, and said unto him, Hear ye me, Asa, and all Judah and Benjamin; The Lord is with you, while ye be with him; and if ye seek him, he will be found of you; but if ye forsake him, he will forsake you" Day 3

(Matthew 7: 7-8) "Ask, and it shall be given you; seek, and ye shall find; knock, and it shall be opened unto you" "For every one that asketh recieveth; and he that seeketh findeth; and to him that knocketh it shall be opened" Day 4

(Acts 15:17) "That the residue of men might seek after the Lord, and all the Gentiles, upon whom my name is called, saith the Lord, who doeth all these things" Day 5

(Proverbs 4:22) "For they are life unto those that find them, and health to all their flesh" Day 6

(Psalm 9: 10) "And they that know thy name will put their trust in thee: for thou, Lord, hast not forsaken them that seek thee" Day 7

(Jeremiah 50:4) "In those days, and in that time, saith the LORD, the children of Israel shall come, they and the children of Judah together, going and weeping: they shall go, and seek the LORD their God" Day 8

(Zechariah 8:21) "And the inhabitants of one city shall go to another, saying, Let us go speedily to pray before the Lord, and to seek the Lord of hosts: I will go also" Day 9

(Psalm 27: 8) "When thou saidst, seek ye my face; my heart said unto thee, Thy face, Lord, will I seek" Day 10

(2 Chronicles 11:16) "And after them out of all the tribes of Israel such as set their hearts to seek the Lord God of Israel came to Jerusalem, to sacrifice unto the Lord God of their fathers" Day 11

(Psalm 17:3) "Thou hast proved mine heart; thou hast visited me in the night; thou hast tried me, and shalt find nothing; I am purposed that my mouth shall not transgress" Day 12

(Psalms 119: 2 & 10) "Blessed are they that keep his testimonies, and that seek him with the whole heart" "With my whole heart have I sought thee: O let me not wander from thy commandments" Day 13

(2 Chronicles 15:2) "And he went out to meet Asa, and said unto him, Hear ye me, Asa, and all Judah and Benjamin; The Lord is with you, while ye be with him; and if ye seek him, he will be found of you; but if ye forsake him, he will forsake you" Day 14

(Matthew 6:33) "But seek ye first the kingdom of God, and his righteousness, and all these things shall be added unto you" Day 15

(Deuteronomy 4: 29) "But if from thence thou shalt seek the Lord thy God, thou shalt find him, if thou seek him with all thy heart and with all thy soul" Day 16

(Psalm 27:4) "One thing have I desired of the Lord, that will I seek after; that I may dwell in the house of the Lord all the days of my life, to behold the beauty of the Lord, and to inquire in his temple" Day 17

(Proverbs 2:5) "Then shalt thou understand the fear of the LORD, and find the knowledge of God" Day 18

90 Day Bible Scriptures (Day 18 thru Day 38)

(Hebrews 11: 6) "But without faith it is impossible to please him: for he that cometh to God must believe that he is, and that he is a rewarder of them that diligently seek him" Day 19

(2 Chronicles 14:4) "And commanded Judah to seek the Lord God of their fathers, and to do the law and the commandment" Day 20

(Daniel 9:3) "And I set my face unto the Lord God, to seek by prayer and supplications, with fasting, and sackcloth, and ashes" Day 21

(1 Chronicles 22: 19) "Now set your heart and your soul to seek the Lord your God; arise therefore, and build ye the sanctuary of the Lord God, to bring the ark of the covenant of the Lord, and the holy vessels of God, into the house that is to be built to the name of the Lord" Day 22

(Isaiah 65:10) "And Sharon shall be a fold of flocks, and the valley of Achor a place for the herds to lie down in, for my people that have sought me" Day 23

(Proverbs 1:28) "Then shall they call upon me, but I will not answer; they shall seek me early, but they shall not find me" Day 24

(Amos 5: 4) "For thus saith the Lord unto the house of Israel, seek ye me, and ye shall live" Day 25

(Psalm 34:10) "The young lions do lack, and suffer hunger: but they who seek the LORD shall not want any good thing" Day 26

(Psalms 40:16) "Let all those that seek thee rejoice and be glad in thee: let such as love thy salvation say continually, The Lord be magnified" Day 27

(Ezra 8: 21) "Then I proclaimed a fast there, at the river of Ahava, that we might afflict ourselves before our God, to seek of him a right way for us, and for our little ones, and for all our substance" Day 28

(Psalm 105:3) "Glory ye in his holy name; let the heart of them rejoice that seek the Lord" Day 29

(Psalm 70:4) "Let all those that seek thee rejoice andbe glad in thee: and let such as love thy salvation say continually, Let God be magnified" Day 30

(Luke 11:9) "And I say unto you, Ask, and it shall be given you; seek, and ye shall find; knock, and it shall be opened unto you" Day 31

(Luke 11:10) "For everyone who asketh receiveth; and that seekth findeth; and to him that knocketh it shall be opened" Day 32

(1 Kings 22: 5) "And Jehoshaphat said unto the king of Israel, Enquire, I pray thee, at the word of the Lord today" Day 33

(Psalm 119:10) " With my whole heart have I sought thee: O let me not wander from thy commandments" Day 34

(Job 11:7) "Canst thou by searching find out God? canst thou find out the Almighty unto perfection?" Day 35

(Romans 2: 7) "To them who by patient continuance in well doing seek for glory and honour and immortality, eternal life" Day 36

(Ezra 8:23) " So we fasted and besought our God for this: and he was intreated of us" Day 37

(1 Chronicles 16:11) "Seek the LORD and his strength, seek his face continually" Day 38

(Proverbs 28: 5) "Evil men understand not judgment: but they that seek the Lord understand all things" Day 39

(Deuteronomy 12:5) "But unto the place which the LORD your God shall choose out of all your tribes to put his name there, even unto his habitation shall ye seek, and thither thou shalt come" Day 40

90 Day Bible Scriptures (Day 39 thru Day 60)

(John 10:9) "I am the door: by me if any man enter in, he shall be saved, and shall go in and out, and find pasture" Day 41

(2 Chronicles 7: 14) "If my people, which are called by my name, shall humble themselves, and pray, and seek my face, and turn from their wicked ways; then I will hear from heaven, and will forgive their sin, and will heal their land" Day 42

(Judges 18:5) "And they said unto him, Ask counsel, we pray thee, of God, that we may know whether our way which we go shall be prosperous" Day 43

(Psalm 77:6) "I call to remembrance my song in the night: I commune with mine own heart: and my spirit made diligent search" Day 44

(Acts 17: 27) "That they should seek the Lord, if haply they might feel after him, and find him, though he be not far from every one of us" Day 45

(2 chronicles 20:4) "And Judah gathered themselves together, to ask help of the LORD: even out of all the cities of Judah they came to seek the LORD" Day 46

(Luke 15:8) "Either what woman having ten pieces of silver, if she lose one piece, doth not light a candle, and sweep the house, and seek diligently till she find it?" Day 47

(Jeremiah 29: 13) "And ye shall seek me, and find me, when ye shall search for me with all your heart" Day 48

(Psalm 139:23) "Search me, O God, and know my heart: try me, and know my thoughts" Day 49

(Ecclesiastes 7:25) "I applied mine heart to know, and to search, and to seek out wisdom, and the reason of things, and to know the wickedness of folly, even of foolishness and madness" Day 50

(Isaiah 55: 6) "Seek ye the Lord while he may be found, call ye upon him while he is near" Day 51

(Jeremiah 17:10) "I the LORD search the heart, I try the reins, even to give every man according to his ways, and according to the fruit of his doings" Day 52

(Luke 15:4) "What man of you, having an hundred sheep, if he lose one of them, doth not leave the ninety and nine in the wilderness, and go after that which is lost, until he find it?" Day 53

(Colossians 3: 1-2) "If ye then be risen with Christ, seek those things which are above, where Christ sitteth on the right hand of God" "Set your affection on things above, not on things on the earth" Day 54

(John 5:39) "Search the scriptures; for in them ye think ye have eternal life: and they are they which testify of me" Day 55

(Psalm 139:1) "O lord, thou hast searched me, and known me" Day 56

(Psalm 63: 1) "O God, thou art my God; early will I seek thee: my soul thirsteth for thee, my flesh longeth for thee in a dry and thirsty land, where no water is" Day 57

(Acts 17:11) "These were more noble than those in Thessalonica, in that they received the word with all readiness of mind, and searched the scriptures daily, whether those things were so" Day 58

(1 Peter 1:10) "Of which salvation the prophets have enquired and searched diligently, who prophesied of the grace that should come unto you" Day 59

(Proverbs 8: 17) "I love them that love me; and those that seek me early shall find me" Day 60

(Revelation 3:20) "Behold, I stand at the door, and knock: if any man hear my voice, and open the door, I will come in to him, and will sup with him, and he with me" Day 61

90 Day Bible Scriptures (Day 61 thru Day 80)

(Jeremiah 6:16) "Thus saith the LORD, Stand ye in the ways, and see, and ask for the old paths, where is the good way, and walk therein, and ye shall find rest for your souls. But they said, We will not walk therein" Day 62

(1 Chronicles 16: 10) "Glory ye in his holy name: let the heart of them rejoice that seek the Lord" Day 63

(John 7:34) "Ye shall seek me, and shall not find me: and where I am, thither ye cannot come" Day 64

(Luke 12:37) "Blessed are those servants, whom the lord when he cometh shall find watching: verily I say unto you, that he shall gird himself, and make them to sit down to meat, and will come forth and serve them" Day 65

(Zephaniah 2: 3) "Seek ye the Lord, all ye meek of the earth, which have wrought his judgment; seek righteousness, seek meekness: it may be ye shall be hid in the day of the Lord's anger" Day 66

(Numbers 10:33) "And they departed from the mount of the LORD three days' journey: and the ark of the covenant of the LORD went before them in the three days' journey, to search out a resting place for them" Day 67

(1 Peter 1:11) "Searching what, or what manner of time the Spirit of Christ which was in them did signify, when it testified beforehand the sufferings of Christ, and the glory that should follow" Day 68

(Psalm 14: 2) "The Lord looked down from heaven upon the children of men, to see if there were any that did understand, and seek God" Day 69

(Ezra 8:22) "For I was ashamed to require of the king a band of soldiers and horsemen to help us against the enemy in the way: because we had spoken unto the king, saying, The hand of our God is upon all them for good that seek him; but his power and his wrath is against all them that forsake him" Day 70

(Matthew 16:25) "For whosoever will save his life shall lose it: and whosoever will lose his life for my sake shall find it" Day 71

(Luke 12: 31) "But rather seek ye the kingdom of God; and all these things shall be added unto you" Day 72

(Psalm 77:2) "In the day of my trouble I sought the Lord: my sore ran in the night, and ceased not: my soul refused to be comforted" Day 73

(Psalm 119:94) " I am thine, save me: for I have sought thy precepts" Day 74

(Psalm 69: 32) "The humble shall see this, and be glad: and your heart shall live that seek God" Day 75

(Luke 6:19) "And the whole multitude sought to touch him: for there went virtue out of him, and healed them all" Day 76

(Matthew 11:29) "Take my yoke upon you, and learn of me; for I am meek and lowly in heart: and ye shall find rest unto your souls" Day 77

(Psalm 34: 4) "I sought the Lord, and he heard me, and delivered me from all my fears" Day 78

(Luke 5:18) "And, behold, men brought in a bed a man which was taken with a palsy: and they sought means to bring him in, and to lay him before him" Day 79

(Luke 4:42) "And when it was day, he departed and went into a desert place: and the people sought him, and came unto him, and stayed him, that he should not depart from them" Day 80

(Psalm 1: 2) "But his delight is in the law of the Lord; and in his law doth he meditate day and night" Day 81

90 Day Bible Scriptures (Day 81 thru Day 90)

(2 Chronicles 26:5) "And he sought God in the days of Zechariah, who had understanding in the visions of God: and as long as he sought the LORD, God made him to prosper" Day 82

(Matthew 10:39) "He that findeth his life shall lose it: and he that loseth his life for my sake shall find it"
Day 83

(Luke19:3) "And he sought to see Jesus who he was; and could not for the press, because he was little of stature" Day 84

(2 Timothy 2: 15) "Study to shew thyself approved unto God, a workman that needeth not to be ashamed"
Day 85

(Proverbs 3:13) "Happy is the man that findeth wisdom, and the man that getteth understanding"
Day 86

(Matthew 7:14) "Because strait is the gate, and narrow is the way, which leadeth unto life, and few there be that find it" Day 87

(Psalm 24: 6) "This is the generation of them that seek him, that seek thy face, O Jacob. Selah"
Day 88

(Proverbs 8:35) "For whoso findeth me findeth life, and shall obtain favour of the LORD" Day 89

(Matthew 7: 7-8) "Ask, and it shall be given you; seek, and ye shall find; knock, and it shall be opened unto you" "For every one that asketh recieveth; and he that seeketh findeth; and to him that knocketh it shall be opened" Day 90

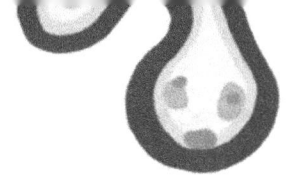

LET'S GET STARTED

KING JAMES VERSION (KJV) BIBLE?

THAT'S Confusing!

NO WORRIES, WE DID THE HARD WORK FOR YOU, GO TO:

www.honeykeepministries.org

AND CLICK ON THE MENU TAB

"Get The Scriptures"

AND DOWNLOAD THE PDF DOCUMENT OF ALL SCRIPTURES FEATURED IN THIS DEVOTIONAL IN AN EASY TO UNDERSTAND TRANSLATION!

Day 1
Seeking God
Read (Hosea 10: 12) KJV

How often do I spend time with God? This is a question that we all must ask ourselves from time to time. Praying and reading God's word along with many other things can be beneficial to our health and well being. God has so many wonderful things in store for us if we just trust and seek Him for advice. He's waiting. let's ALL open the door and let Him in.

Rufus and Clyde and The Stench of Doom

READ (1 CHRONICLES 28:9) KJV

Introducing Rufus Wyde! Below are some things about Rufus. It's good to know things about people because friendships can blossom. You discover things that you share in common. **What do you think about having God for a friend? He loves who you love, including yourself. He likes who you are, so you don't have to change. He even enjoys what you enjoy. Do you think that sounds like a friend?** Ask in prayer, seek through the scriptures and find out for yourself.

FIRST NAME:	RUFUS
LAST NAME:	WYDE
PARENTS:	MR. & MRS. WYDE
AGE:	9
ADDRESS:	42 SAND STREET IN MANNA'S VILLE
SCHOOL:	MANNA'S VILLE ELEMENTARY
GRADE:	4TH
BEST FRIEND:	CLYDE PALMS
HOBBIES:	PLAYING VIDEO GAMES, PRANKING NEIGHBORS AND PLAYING OUTSIDE WITH FRIENDS.
GOALS:	BECOMING THE HOT DOG KING CHAMPION IN THE ALL-YOU-CAN-EAT MANNA'S VILLE FAIR CONTEST, AND DOING WELL IN SCHOOL SO HE CAN COMPETE IN THE COMPETITION.

Enjoy!

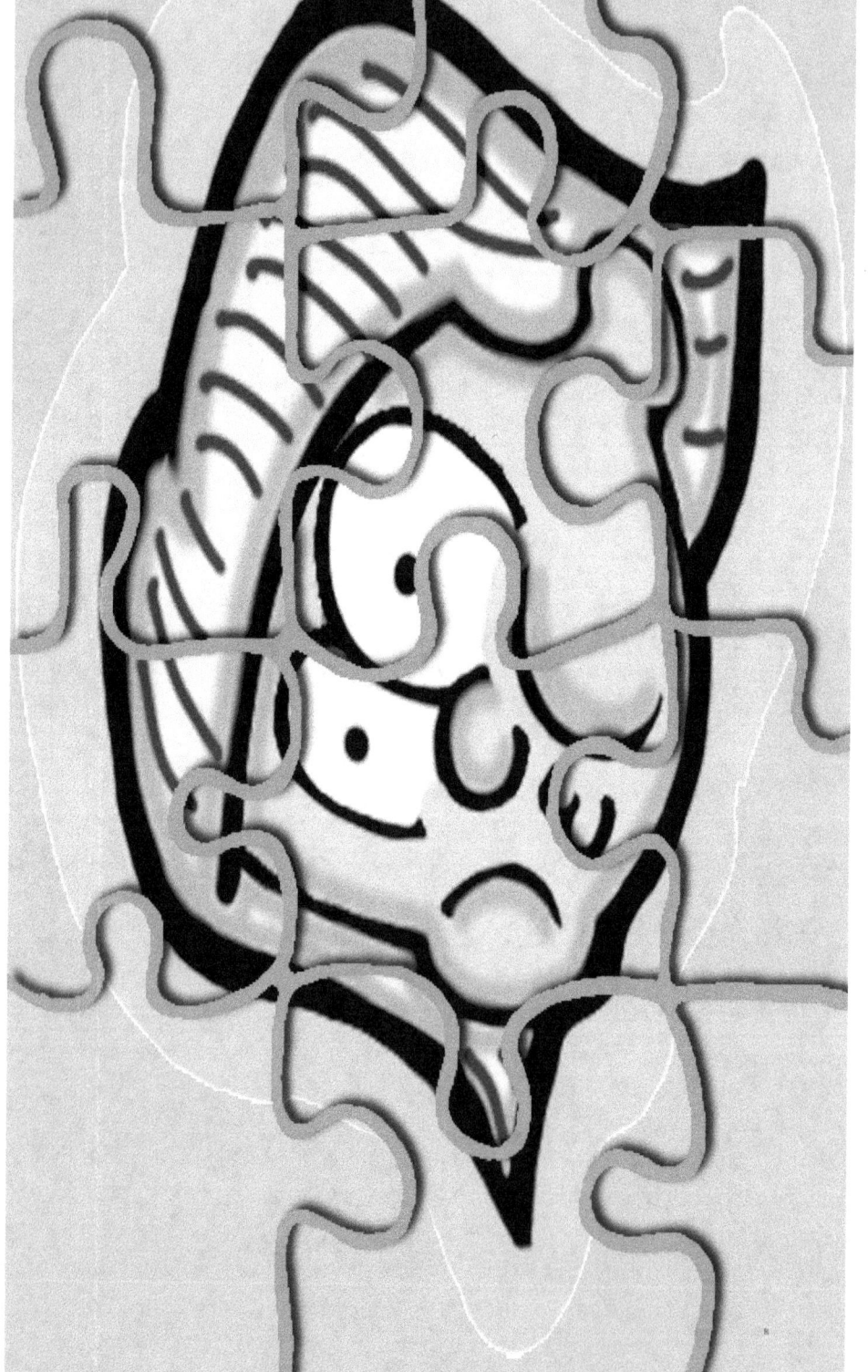

Meeting The Characters:

"And he_____out to meet Asa, and said unto him, Hear ye me, Asa, and all Judah and Benjamin; The_____is with you, while ye be with him; and if ye_____him, he will be found of you;_____if ye forsake him, he will forsake you"

CLYDE PALMS

FIRST NAME: CLYDE

LAST NAME: PALMS

PARENTS: MR. & MRS. PALMS

AGE: 9

ADDRESS: 90 CACTUS ROAD IN MANNA'S VILLE

SCHOOL: MANNA'S VILLE ELEMENTARY

GRADE: 4TH

BEST FRIEND: RUFUS WYDE

HOBBIES: PLAYING SPORTS WITH FRIENDS, TRAINING AND PLAYING WITH HIS PET SHEEP HOWARD AND WATCHING T.V.

GOALS: BECOMING AN ALL AROUND ATHLETE, DO GOOD IN SCHOOL AND CHANGE THE SCHOOL SYSTEM WHERE PETS CAN COME TO SCHOOL AND LEARN TOO!

Rufus and Clyde and The Stench of Doom

Sleep over Mayhem was on the brain when Rufus arrived home with friend Clyde after school was over. Both boys rushed out of the car while Clyde's mom waved a farewell goodbye as they ran to the door where Rufus's mom stood welcoming them in. They quickly removed their hats and coats and flung them on the coat rack. Not a moment more could be wasted on anything other than their agenda for this special Friday afternoon. The boys had it all planned out to perfection.

Later on that evening in Rufus bedroom, the two boys rested in fulfillment from their busy day.

They left no stone unturned on this epic sleep over. Both wore their costume moustaches to bed as a reminder of the moustache prank on Mr. Lee's old guard dog Sheila and herd of sheep. Their bellies were full enough to burst from all of the pizza and wings they consumed during their all-you-can-eat contest. Their fingers were numb from all of the video games they played and competed in. And their minds were tired from all the creepy make believe stories they shared before they crashed for tonight. And in the mist of their fulfilling day, they talked with Rufus mom about the "Asking, Seeking and Knocking" scripture (Matthew 7:7-8) they learned in school. She was so impressed that she decided to get them tacos for tomorrow...............

READ *(Matthew 7: 7-8)* KJV **AND FILL IN THE BLANK WORDS:**

"_____, and it shall be given;_____, and ye shall find;_____, and it shall be_____unto you. For every one that_____ recieveth; and he that seeketh_____; and to him that knocketh it shall be_____"

WOW, Rufus and Clyde were all about planning mischief today.

What's on your "To Do List"?

Are you helping with chores? Starting or completing your homework? Reading your bible or praying? Why don't you fill out the "To Do List" as a reminder so you won't forget

My
"TO DO List"

Morning
1.
2.
3.
4.
5.
6.

Evening
1.
2.
3.
4.
5.
6.

Night
1.
2.
3.
4.
5.
6.

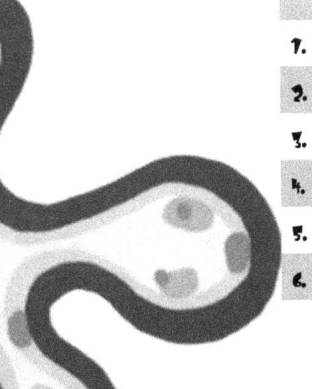

GReat JOb!

Rufus and Clyde and The Stench of Doom

Day 5 READING OLYMPIC'S CHALLENGE:

Read Acts 15:17 KJV and fill in the missing words:

"That the residue of_____might seek after the_____, and all the Gentiles, upon whom my_____is called, saith the Lord, who doeth_____these things"

Have you asked God for anything today?
One thing is for sure, He's asking us to spend a little time with Him each and everyday, Amen!

CHALLENGE:

Here's a little bit of yesterday's story. Challenge yourself by reading the story UP-SIDE DOWN?

..........."They left no stone unturned on this epic sleep over. Both wore their costume moustaches to bed as a reminder of the moustache prank on Mr. Lee's old guard dog Sheila and herd of sheep. Their bellies were full enough to burst from all of the pizza and wings they consumed during their all-you-can-eat contest. Their fingers were numb from all of the video games they played and competed in. And their minds were tired from all the creepy make believe stories they shared before they crashed for tonight......

Well Done!

Rufus and Clyde and The Stench of Doom

Read (Proverbs 4:22) KJV

"For they are life unto those that FIND them, and health to all their flesh"

Have you ever had a day go as planned like Rufus and Clyde's? We all have, especially if our secret weapon is prayer. SEEKing GOD's direction for the day always brings Good results!

GETTING BACK TO THE STORY . . . .
HERE ARE SOME CLUES TO WHAT'S COMING UP:

Sleeping Bags?   Blame?   Room?

Scent?

What do you think is going to happen?
SEEK out some ideas while you play a card game with the cards on the following 4 pages:

1. Cut them out. 2. Mix them up. 3. Place them face down.
4. Match all the cards that are alike.

PLAY CARDS! GOOD GAME!

Rufus and Clyde and The Stench of Doom

Make sure you keep your cards to play again and again **when it's time! Enjoy!**

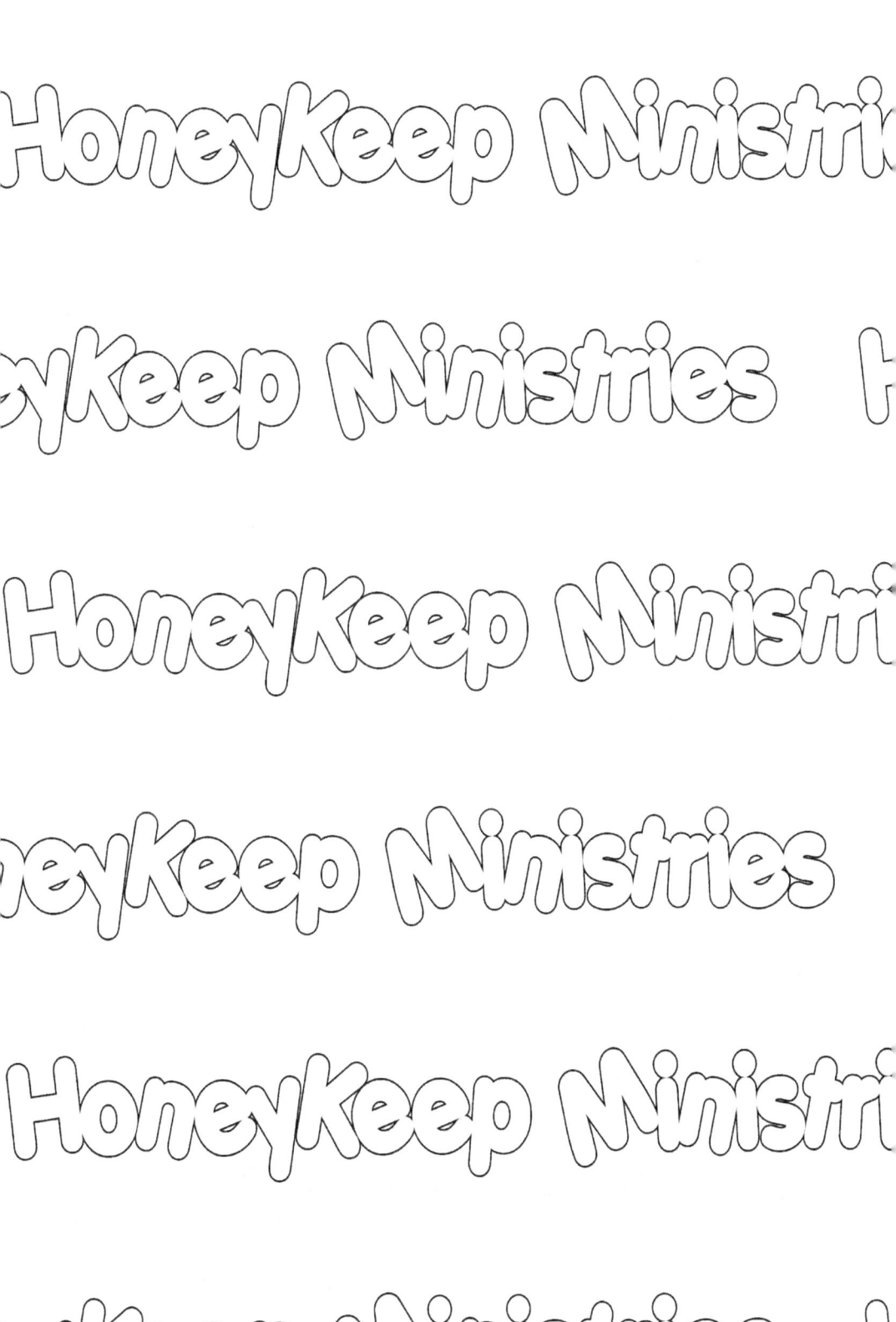

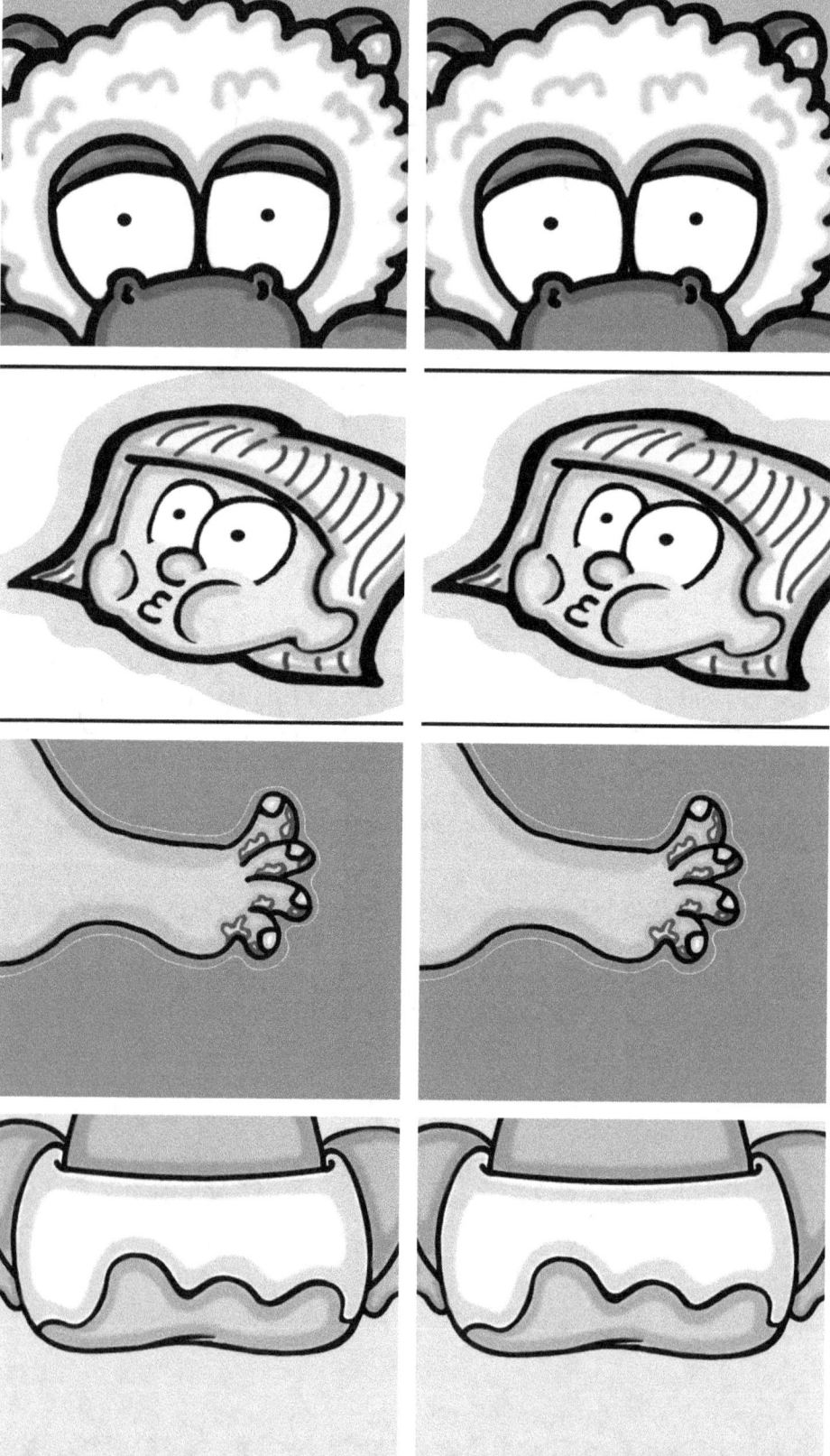

HoneyKeep Ministries

HoneyKeep Ministries

HoneyKeep Ministries

HoneyKeep Ministries

HoneyKeep Ministries

HoneyKeep Ministries

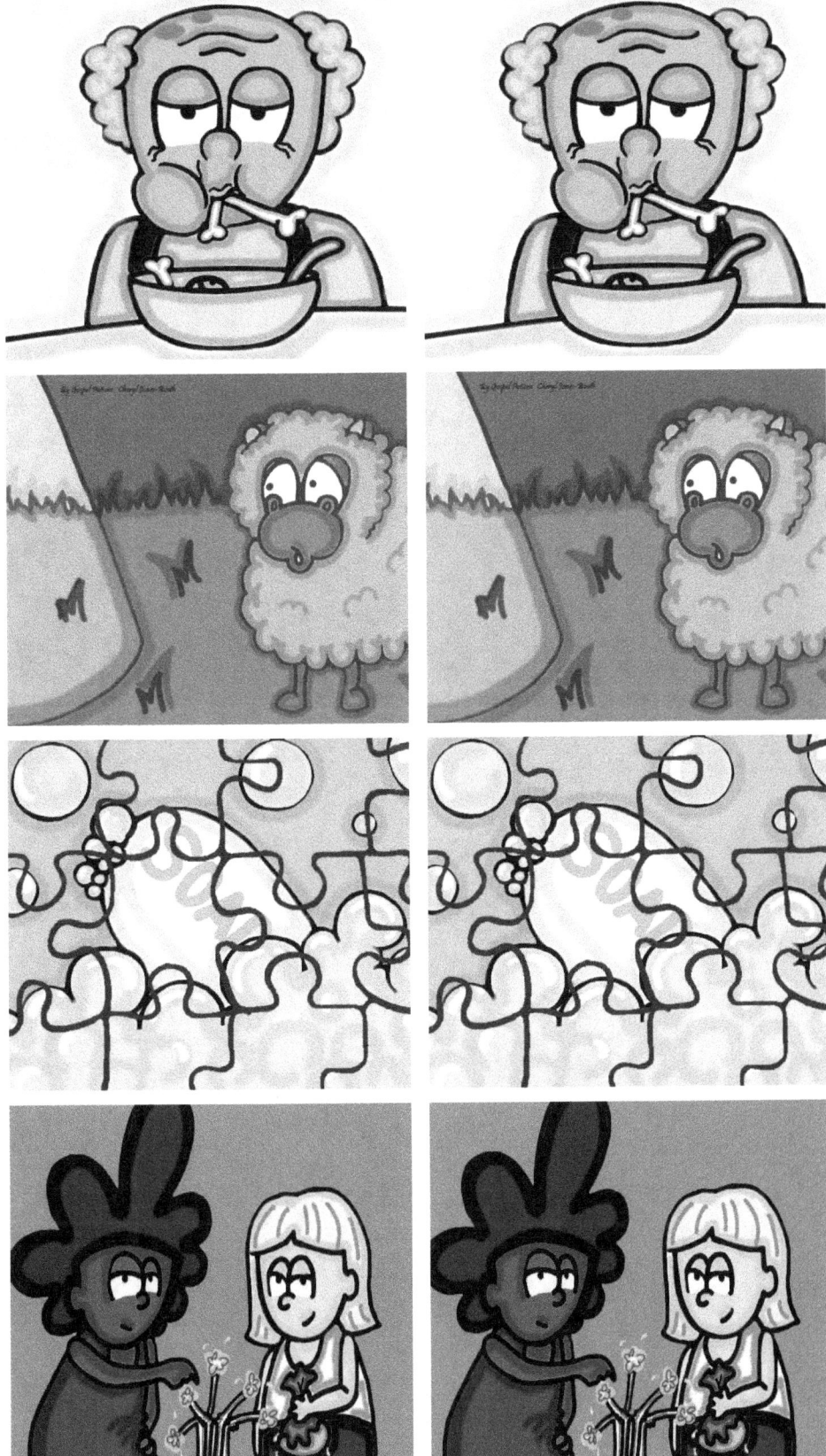

HoneyKeep Minist

eyKeep Ministries

HoneyKeep Minist

neyKeep Ministries

HoneyKeep Minist

eyKeep Ministries

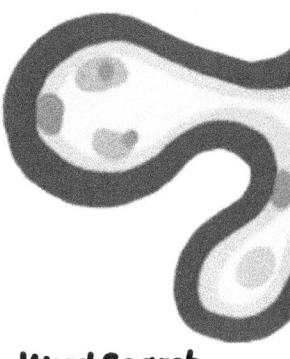

...........The only thing left to do now was to sleep and dream of great tasting tacos, so the boys set on a mission to do just that. But their tasty dreaming would be short lived, because something disturbing began to fill the air. It was like a nasty mixture of gym socks, corn chips, farts, rotten food, garbage and skunks. The boys stood up from their sleeping bags in disgust!

"You passed gas!" Rufus screamed as he pointed at Clyde while holding his nose.

"No, it was you who passed gas!".....................

READ (PSALM 9:10) KJV

Word Search List:

- rotten
- Matthew
- Far
- Job
- cornchips
- Exodus
- Smell
- Joel
- our
- Psalm
- Skunk
- Bible

R	O	T	T	E	N	H	J	B	O	A	L	N	M
P	Y	M	G	P	Y	Z	U	J	D	S	G	S	W
J	F	M	A	T	T	H	E	W	E	K	C	M	I
A	C	P	F	U	Q	L	J	K	O	S	Y	E	H
F	A	R	T	Y	B	D	N	F	X	O	U	L	N
J	P	K	D	L	K	I	A	H	M	U	B	L	R
E	C	J	O	B	T	Q	B	P	H	R	X	Y	D
X	Z	J	Y	U	B	Y	E	L	Q	F	M	L	J
O	F	K	G	S	K	P	K	L	W	L	C	K	O
D	P	B	K	N	G	H	G	S	A	O	Q	X	E
U	D	L	U	Q	X	Z	F	S	D	I	Z	R	L
S	X	K	H	N	Y	O	P	J	U	V	B	K	T
H	S	V	C	O	R	N	C	H	I	P	S	H	M

Rufus and Clyde and The Stench of Doom

Day 8 Can You Remember . . . .

READ JEREMIAH 50:4 KJV

PEE YEW, what smells so bad? Maybe Rufus or Clyde did
pass gas and didn't say "excuse me", how rude.
Speaking of being rude, did you say your prayers today?
It would be rude of us to go throughout our day and not
knock on Heaven's door for Godly answers, Amen!

Let's see how good your memory is from yesterday's story:

1. WHAT FOOD WAS RUFUS AND CLYDE DREAMING ABOUT?

A. TACOS
B. CHEESE BURGERS
C. CANDY
D. PIZZA

2. NAME THREE THINGS THE ODOR SMELLED LIKE?

A. HAIRSPRAY, COFFEE, GRASS
B. PERFUME, CANDLES, IN-SCENTS
C. GYM SOCKS, FARTS, SKUNKS
D. SPOILED MILK, ONIONS, GARLIC

3. WHAT WAS RUFUS AND CLYDE DOING?

A. PLAYING VIDEO GAMES
B. SLEEPING
C. WATCHING T.V.
D. PLAYING OUTSIDE

4. WHO DID RUFUS AND CLYDE BLAME THE SMELL ON?

A. A NEIGHBOR
B. A GHOST
C. A PET
D. EACH OTHER

Well Done!

Rufus and Clyde and The Stench of Doom

CAN YOU DRAW?

Read (ZECHARIAH 8:21) KJV and fill in the missing words:

"And the inhabitants of one_____shall go to another, saying, Let us go speedily to_____before the Lord, and to_____the Lord of hosts: I will go_____"

We'll find out tomorrow if Rufus and Clyde was successful in seeking out that horrible smell. Maybe they'll stay up all night and try their hardest to search it out. Let's ALL follow their lead and try our hardest in seeking Christ through prayer and serving Him today, Amen! Speaking of trying hard, why don't you take the time and try your hardest to draw Clyde!

◄ DRAW MY PICTURE!

Rufus and Clyde and The Stench of Doom

Day 10

..........Rufus opened up the window and stuck his head out, Clyde quickly ran over to do the same. Sweet relief filled their nostrils as they breathed in the surrounding fresh air. Assuming the odor has pass, they both leaned back in and closed the window. To their surprise; the smell was still present. This stench was something that needed to be thrown out..................

Read (Psalm 27: 8) *KJV* and fill in the missing words within the scripture

"When_____saidst,_____ye   my_____;   my _____said unto_____, Thy face,_____, will I seek"

Hopefully Rufus and Clyde will get to the bottom of this stink fast! Prayer would be a useful KEY in their quest.
Below cross out all the stinky things unrelated to Christ:

Dirty Socks	Christ	High Priest
Wonderful Counselor	Alpha	Old Cheese
Prince of Peace	Skunk	Shepard
Sour Sneakers	Boiled Eggs	Carpenter
Yahweh	Fish	Spoiled Milk
Savior	I Am	Jesus
Spoiled Food	Omega	Abba
Garbage	Father	Bad Breath

EXCELLENT WORK!

Rufus and Clyde and The Stench of Doom

Read (2 CHRONICLES 11:16) KJV and fill in the missing words:

"And after them out of_____ the tribes of Israel such as set their hearts to_____ the Lord God of Israel_____ to Jerusalem, to sacrifice unto the Lord God of their_____"

What did you receive out of today's scripture? Hopefully it was something peaceful and satisfying. Sort of like Rufus and Clyde sticking their heads out of the window to get away from that sticky odor! Yikes!

CHALLENGE:

Here's some of yesterday's story. Challenge yourself by reading it CIRCLE style?

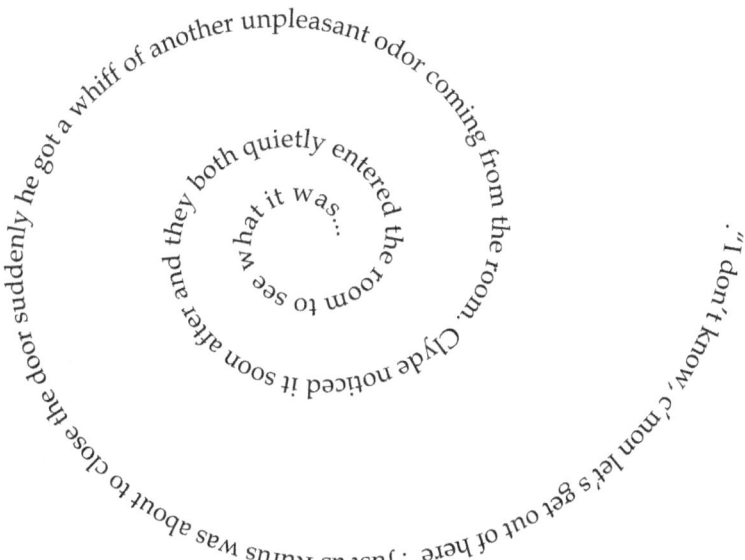

Rufus and Clyde and The Stench of Doom

Day 12

Yuck!

Read (Psalm 17:3) KJV

"Thou hast proved mine heart; thou hast visited me in the night; thou hast tried me, and shalt **FIND** nothing; I am purposed that my mouth shall not transgress"

Have you ever played hide and seek? Its fun to play, especially when you find a great hiding spot where no one can find you. But when it comes to God, He doesn't like when we hide from Him. He wants us to willingly come and seek His face openly. Amen.

Clues:

LIGHT SWITCH

Getting Back To The Story,
To the right are some clues to what's coming up:

BED

What do you think is going to happen?

CLOSET

SEEK OUT SOME IDEAS WHILE YOU PLAY A MEMORY CARD GAME WITH THE CARDS THAT YOU CUT OUT PREVIOUSLY (FROM DAY 6)!

SEARCH

1. Mix them up. 2. Place them face down.
3. Match all the cards that are alike.

TOYS

Rufus and Clyde and The Stench of Doom

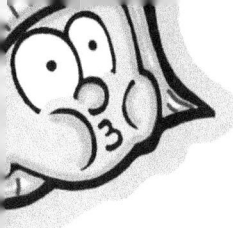
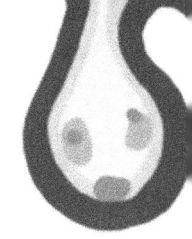

Day 13

…………...They turned on the light and began to search. They looked under the bed, behind the mountain of toys, in the closet and under the dresser drawers. They searched high and low for this dreadful odor. Unfortunately; they had little success. They only discovered a couple dirty socks and under garments, candy wrappers, a few half eaten chicken wings and used gum. Then Clyde had an idea.

"Let's check outside the room, maybe the smell is coming from out there"....................

Read (Psalms 119: 2) KJV

WHEN YOU'RE SEARCHING FOR A TROUBLING THING IT TAKES THE TOOLS OF GOD TO LEAD YOU, PLUS SOME FAITH IN THE MATTER THAT HE WILL WORK IT OUT!
DECSRIBE BELOW WHAT THESE COMMON CHRIST SEEKING TOOLS MEAN TO YOU:

Reading My Bible means to me

Praying to God means to me

Having Faith means to me.....

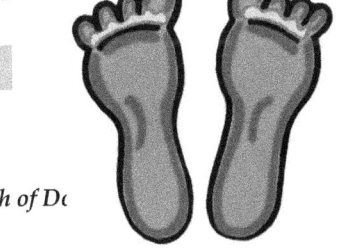

Rufus and Clyde and The Stench of D(

Day 14

CAN YOU REMEMBER.....

Read (2 Chronicles 15:12) KJV and fill in the Missing words:

"And they entered_____a covenant to_____the Lord God of their_____with all their_____and with all their soul"

EVER FEEL LIKE GIVING UP ON SOMETHING? I'M SURE RUFUS AND CLYDE FEEL LIKE GIVING UP ON WHAT'S CAUSING THIS SMELL. JUST REMEMBER, GOD IS ALWAYS THERE FOR US WHENEVER WE NEED A HELPING HAND. ALL WE HAVE TO DO IS SEEK HIS FACE AND TRUST HE'LL HAVE THE ANSWER.

LET'S SEE HOW GOOD YOUR MEMORY IS FROM YESTERDAY'S STORY:

WHO'S IDEA WAS IT TO SEARCH OUTSIDE THE ROOM?

A. CLYDE
B. RUFUS
C. MR. WYDE (RUFUS DAD)
D. MRS. WYDE (RUFUS MOM)

WHERE WAS SOME PLACES RUFUS AND CLYDE LOOKED FOR THE SMELL?

A. BEHIND THE T.V. AND UNDER A BLANKET
B. IN THE LAUNDRY BASKET AND IN A BOX
C. IN THE KITCHEN AND IN THE BATHROOM
D. UNDER THE BED AND IN THE CLOSET.

WHAT DID RUFUS AND CLYDE FIND WHEN SEARCHING FOR THE SMELL?

A. SUNGLASSES, HATS AND GLOVES
B. USED TOOTH BRUSH, TISSUE AND PAPER
C. DIRTY SOCKS, UNDER GARMENTS AND USED GUM
D. CHIPS, BROCCOLI AND SPINACH

WHAT DID RUFUS AND CLYDE TURN ON TO SEARCH FOR THE ODOR?

A. A FLASHLIGHT
B. THE LIGHT SWITCH
C. THE T.V.
D. THE CELL PHONE

Rufus and Clyde and The Stench of Doom

Can You Draw? **DAY 15**

Read **Matthew 6:33** KJV

Tomorrow you will read a little more of the story. Can you guess what's going to happen when Rufus and Clyde leave the room.? There are so many possibilities. One thing is for sure, God knows ALL because He's All Knowing. Let's all think about that when we seek His face in prayer.

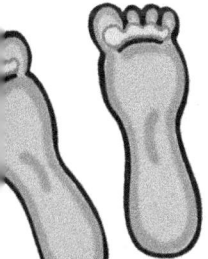 ◄ Can you draw these feet?

Rufus and Clyde and The Stench of Doom

Day 16

..............So they ventured outside of Rufus room. Clyde brought a flashlight to help guide the way through the dimly lit home. Everyone was asleep to their knowledge and they did not want to wake anyone up.

"Where should we go first?" Clyde whispered.

"Let's go to the kitchen"

"Good idea"

So they headed towards the kitchen. Sadly Rufus mom had a bad reputation of being a poor cook. Her meals were often difficult to swallow and rarely did anyone ask for seconds. Oftentimes prepared dishes go days without being touched again before being thrown out for garbage. Perhaps something spoiled and just needed to be thrown away. So they tip toed towards the kitchen in hopes of discovering where the smell was.................

READ
(Deut. 4:29)

Rufus and Clyde's journey is now leading them to the kitchen. When you are seeking God about something how do you pray? Write down your prayer to God in the space to the right

My Special prayer.......

_____

_____

_____

_____

_____

_____

_____

_____

_____

In Jesus Name, Amen

Rufus and Clyde and The Stench of Doom

Read (Psalm 27:4) KJV and fill in the missing words:

"One thing_____I desired of the Lord, that will I_____after; that I may dwell in the_____of the Lord all the_____of my life, to behold the beauty of the Lord,_____to inquire in his temple"

CHALLENGE:

HERE'S SOME OF YESTERDAY'S STORY. CHALLENGE YOURSELF BY READING IT "MAZE STYLE":

▲ ...So they ventured outside of Rufus room. Clyde brought a flashlight to help guide the way through the dimly lit home. "Where should we go first?" Clyde whispered. Let's go to the kitchen. "Good idea" So they headed towards the kitchen. Sadly Rufus mom had a bad reputation of being a poor cook. Her meals were often difficult to swallow and rarely did any -one ask for seconds. Oftentimes prepared......

Rufus and Clyde and The Stench of Doom

Day 18

Read (Proverbs 2:5) KJV

"Then shalt thou understand the fear of the LORD, and **find** the knowledge of God"

EEWWW, which is worst! Dealing with a horrible smell, or having to eat someone's bad cooking? Poor Rufus and Clyde, hopefully they've said their prayers today. It looks like their going to need it.
What about you, have you read your bible or said your daily prayers today? I hope so. You never know if you'll end up like poor Rufus and Clyde!

HERE ARE SOME CLUES TO WHAT'S COMING UP IN TOMORROW'S TALE:

SOUR HAM

THE FRIDGE

UPSIDE DOWN CAKE

EYEBALL AND BONE STEW

What do you think is going to happen in tomorrow's story?

Seek OUT SOME IDEAS WHILE YOU PLAY A MEMORY CARD GAME WITH THE CARDS THAT YOU CUT OUT PREVIOUSLY
(FROM **DAY 6**)!

1. **Mix them up.** 2. **Place them face down.**
3. **Match all the cards that are alike.**

Rufus and Clyde and The Stench of Doom

Day 19

……………They opened the refrigerator door and to their horror they could see all the leftovers Mrs. Wyde had made throughout the week. The chicken pot pie casserole had feathers sticking out of the dish. The beef stew had eyeballs and bones floating inside the stew. The honey ham looked more like sour ham. The buttered biscuits were as hard as a rock. And the upside down cake was really upside down! The boys almost fainted in disgust, if it wasn't for Rufus realizing something. This was only painful to look at but not to smell. The stench was lurking elsewhere.....................

READ (Hebrews 11: 6) KJV AND FILL IN THE MISSING WORDS.

"But without_____it is impossible to_____Him: for he that cometh to_____must believe that_____is, and that He is a_____of them that diligently_____Him"

WOW, RUFUS AND CLYDE WERE RIGHT; SHE CAN'T COOK AND MAY BE BEHIND THIS HORRIBLE STENCH. **BELOW IS A LIST OF INGREDIENTS NEEDED FOR SERVING CHRIST. CONNECT WHAT MATCHES AND LEAVE WHAT DOES NOT.**

Church	Worship
Apple	House of God
Shepard	Granola
Crust	Bake 30 Minutes
Praise	Bible
Cinnamin	Dough
Fruit of the Spirit	Peaches
Yeast	Love, Joy, Peace
God's Word	Preacher

Rufus and Clyde and The Stench of Doom

Day 20 Put On Your Thinking Caps!

Read **2 Chronicles 14:4 KJV** and fill in the missing words:

"And commanded Judah to_____the Lord God of_____
fathers,_____to do the law and the commandment"

Eyeballs in Beef Stew, what was Rufus mom thinking?
Perhaps eyeballs and bones are full of vitamins to help you grow big
and strong. Here's an idea, let's pray that Rufus mom will never make
this dish again! AMEN!

Thinking Cap Time! Here are some questions from yesterday's story:

What room was Rufus and Clyde in?
A. Living Room   B. Basement   C. Kitchen   D. Bedroom

The Chicken Pot Pie Casserole had what inside of it?
A. Feathers   B. Chicken   C. Rice   D. Legs

The Buttered Biscuits were like what?
A. Fluffy Soft   B. Hard as a Rock   C. Lightly toasted
D. Moldy Green

What desert did Rufus and Clyde find Upside Down?
A. The Apple Pie   B. The Jell-O   C. The Rice Pudding
D. The Cake

Rufus and Clyde and The Stench of Doom

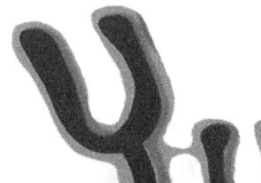

Create A Work-of-Art!

Day 21

Read (Daniel 9:3) KJV

SO WE KNOW THE SMELL IS NOT COMING FROM RUFUS ROOM OR HIS MOM'S POOR COOKING! I CAN'T IMAGINE ANYTHING MORE HORRIBLE, CAN YOU? WE'LL ND OUT MORE TOMORROW. IN THE MEANTIME, LET'S STAY FOCUSED ON SEEKING GOD. NOT JUST FOR RUFUS AND CLYDE'S SAKE, BUT FOR OURSELVES AS WELL.

◄ Can you draw a whole pot of Eyeball and Bone Beef Stew?

Rufus and Clyde and The Stench of Doom

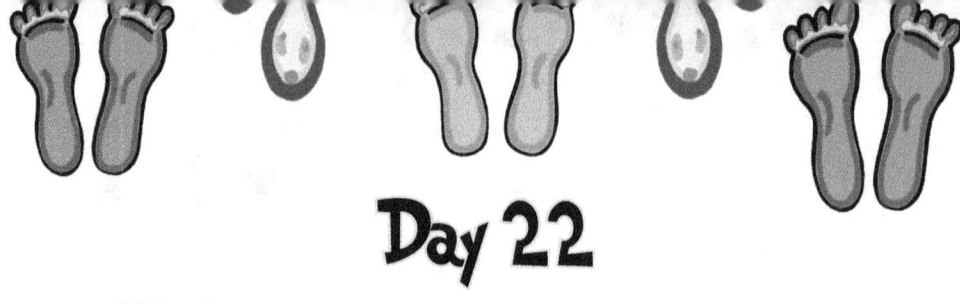

Day 22

"What's going on?"

GASP!! The boys quickly turned in fright as they threw their backs against the
refrigerator door. It was dark in the kitchen and the flashlight laid on the kitchen counter more than an arm stretch away. Both were frozen in fear and could not make a move towards the flashlight to see who this person was. The figure started moving towards them, the
mysterious person flicked on the light. It was Rufus's mom. They sighed in relief but the
terror had yet to pass. Mrs. Wyde was angry, and she wanted to get to the bottom of this.

"Rufus and Clyde what are you two doing? Have you both been playing in the kitchen and experimenting, what is that horrible smell?"........................

READ *(1 Chronicles 22: 19) KJV* **AND FILL IN THE MISSING WORDS**

"Now set your_____and your soul to_____the Lord your God; arise therefore, and build ye the_____of the Lord God, to bring the_____ of the covenant of the_____, and the_____vessels of God, into the_____that is to be built to the_____of the Lord"

It looks like Rufus and Clyde are not the only ones in search of this horrible odor. Perhaps a good idea would be to put their heads together and think of a plan. Rufus's mom may just have some ideas that might help in the discovery. A plan can be helpful in many ways, it can help you shape your day and give you a check list on things that need to be done. Take a moment now and plan out your day with the "My Planner" on the following page:

Rufus and Clyde and The Stench of Doom

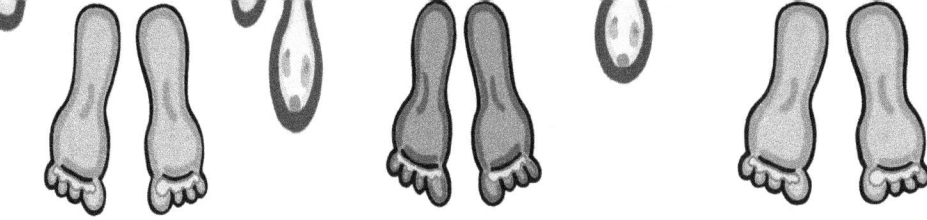

"MY PLANNER"

MORNING

1.
2.
3.
4.
5.
6.

EVENING

1.
2.
3.
4.
5.
6.

NIGHT

1.
2.
3.
4.
5.
6.

Rufus and Clyde and The Stench of Doom

READ (Isaiah 65:10) KJV AND FILL IN THE MISSING WORDS:

"_____Sharon shall be a fold of flocks, and_____valley of Achor a place for the herds to lie_____in, for my people that have sought me"

OUR TWO DETECTIVES ARE IN ALOT OF TROUBLE, HOPEFULLY THEY WILL GET OUT OF IT. LET'S PRAY AND SEEK GOD SO THAT RUFUS AND CLYDE WILL NOT BE IN TOO MUCH TROUBLE, AMEN!

Reading Challenge Today: See if you can read this MIRROR style!

"What's going on?"

GASP!! The boys quickly turned in fright as they threw their backs against the refrigerator door. It was dark in the kitchen and the flashlight laid on the kitchen counter more than an arm stretch away. Both were frozen in fear and could not make a move towards the flashlight to see who this person was. The figure started moving towards them, the mysterious person flicked on the light. It was Rufus's mom. They sighed in relief but the terror had yet to pass. Mrs. Wyde was angry, and she wanted to get to the bottom of this.

"Rufus and Clyde what are you two doing? Have you both been playing in the kitchen and experimenting, what is that horrible smell?........................"

Hint: Place backward words above in front of a mirror and watch the words appear normal again!

Excellent!

Rufus and Clyde and The Stench of Doom

Day 24

"Then shall they call upon me, but I will not answer; they shall seek me early, but they shall not FIND me"

Seeking God might seem like a BIG thing to do. But it's really simple, all we have to do is talk to God and give HIm thanks each and everyday. Speaking of seeking, below is listed some clues to tomorrow's story. What do you think is going to happen? Why don't you think it over while playing a game of "Memory Cards"

Lesson   **"Ask, Seek & Knock"**

Bible Scripture   **Game**

1. MIX THEM UP. 2. PLACE THEM FACE DOWN.
3. MATCH ALL THE CARDS THAT ARE ALIKE.

Rufus and Clyde and The Stench of Doom

Day 25

.........."No we're not doing anything mom, we're trying to find what smells too"

"Ugh yeah, we were just looking around"

Then Mrs. Wyde had an idea. Earlier that day when she talked with the boys about the meaning of the "Ask, Seek and Knock" scripture they learned about in school, they said it sounded like playing "hide and seek" and telling "knock knock" jokes put together. So she decided to use this smelly incident as a way of hopefully explaining what the scripture really means.

"Well it looks like you can cross the kitchen off your list" as she reached for the air freshener on the kitchen counter. "Hey, I got an idea for you both, why don't you and Clyde here start asking some questions in addition to your searching. You know, like detectives"

"Hey mom that's a good idea"

"Yeah" Both their eyes lit up in excitement..............

READ (Amos 5: 4) KJV

"Asking" means to me.........

~~~~~~~~~~~~

~~~~~~~~~~~~

~~~~~~~~~~~~

~~~~~~~~~~~~

"Seeking" means to me........

~~~~~~~~~~~~

~~~~~~~~~~~~

~~~~~~~~~~~~

~~~~~~~~~~~~

"knocking" means to me....

~~~~~~~~~~~~

~~~~~~~~~~~~

~~~~~~~~~~~~

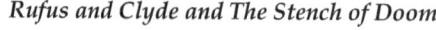

Rufus and Clyde and The Stench of Doom

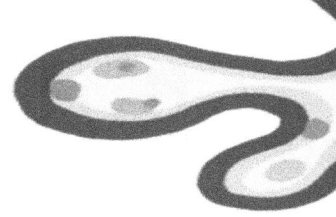

Day 26

Read (Psalm 34:10) KJV and fill in the missing words:

"The young_____do lack, and suffer hunger:_____they who
seek the LORD shall not_____any good thing"

When we lose something special, we look for it. And if we can't find it, it makes
us upset! Thank goodness we can never lose God, He's always near.
Just waiting for us to seek Him out by calling His name.
Let's see how much you remember of yesterday's story:

WHO WAS RUFUS AND CLYDE TALKING TO IN THE KITCHEN?
A. RUFUS COUSIN   **B. RUFUS MOM**   **C. RUFUS SISTER**   **D. RUFUS GRANDPA**

WHAT WAS THE SCRIPTURE MRS. WYDE USED FOR THE GAME?
A. BROTHERLY LOVE   **B. ARMOR OF GOD**   **C. THE BEATTITUDES**
D. ASK, SEEK & KNOCK

WHAT DID RUFUS & CLYDE THINK THE SCRIPTURE MEANT?
A. KNOCK KNOCK JOKES   **B.** WISDOM   **C.** DON'T BE BAD   **D.** BE A NICE PERSON

keep up the GOOD work!!!

Rufus and Clyde and The Stench of Doom

Day 27

Read (Psalms 40:16) KJV

Saying good morning when you wake up, and goodnight before going to bed to your loved ones means that you care. We can do the same when we pray to God everyday!

CAN YOU DRAW
RUFUS HEAD? →

Rufus and Clyde and The Stench of Doom

Day 28

...........She filled them in on what she thought could be the stench. She mentioned the leftovers that may have went bad in the frig, however they informed her that they already looked there. She told them about the backyard garbage can that needed to be cleaned out for weeks; but she finally cleaned it out just yesterday. She couldn't think of anything else that could be the cause.

"Hmm, I just don't know. Try starting your search with Grandpa, and don't you two stay up too late"

"Okay, we won't" they replied as they ran out of the kitchen straight to Grandpa Morris room............

Read (Ezra 8: 27) KJV

Word Search List:
- Mildew
- Joseph
- Stink
- Mary
- Gas
- Noah
- Odor
- Moses
- Ghastly
- Abraham
- Foul
- Jesus

HMMM; GRANDPA MORRIS JUST MIGHT BE THE PERSON RUFUS & CLYDE ARE SEARCHING FOR AFTER ALL.

SPEAKING OF SEARCHING, WHY DON'T YOU TAKE THE TIME TO SEARCH OUT ALL THE WORDS AND BIBLE PEOPLE IN THE WORD SEARCH BELOW.

G	F	C	X	L	H	U	I	P	M	O	S	E	S
D	S	T	I	N	K	F	A	Z	X	J	I	B	N
J	G	F	Y	T	A	U	G	H	A	S	T	L	Y
O	D	G	M	C	J	B	U	G	C	X	S	K	T
S	D	R	N	G	W	X	R	S	N	O	A	H	K
E	F	J	E	S	U	S	I	A	C	J	T	D	M
P	D	A	Y	H	E	G	N	U	H	X	I	F	W
H	X	B	C	U	U	Y	M	Z	D	A	P	W	G
U	M	I	L	D	E	W	R	Z	G	H	M	O	A
O	W	A	N	K	Y	D	F	U	Y	K	G	D	S
J	D	K	U	U	D	E	S	R	F	P	Q	J	B
A	M	O	F	X	W	J	A	T	G	M	O	U	L
C	I	J	R	D	U	M	K	Q	D	H	B	R	X

YOU Did It!

Rufus and Clyde and The Stench of Doom

Day 29

Read (Psalm 105:3) KJV and fill in the missing words:

"Glory ye in his_____name; let the heart of _____rejoice
that_____the Lord"

Just think, Rufus and Clyde may be solving the mystery pretty soon.
So long bad smells! Your reign of nose terror is almost at its end.
Did you know that being bad or not listening has a nasty smell of its own?
It does, when we don't act Christ like it smells bad to God.
So let's all make sure we seek His face in prayer and do His will.

Here's some of yesterday's story. Challenge yourself by reading it **CIRCLE** style?

a whiff of another unpleasant odor coming from the room. Clyde noticed it soon after and they both quietly entered the room to see what it was... "I don't know,' c'mon let's get out of here." Just as Rufus was about to close the door suddenly he got

Rufus and Clyde and The Stench of Doom

Day 30

"Seeking God"

Read (Psalms 70: 4) KJV

There are many things in life that we take for granted. One of those many things is Christ. Whether we pray to Him or not, He still loves us very much and waits patiently for us to spend quality time with Him. Thank God He is a patient and loving Father. Let's not keep Him waiting any longer, let's get on our knees and seek His Face for direction.

Rufus and Clyde and The Stench of Doom

Day 31

READ **(Luke 11:9) KJV** AND FILL IN THE MISSING WORDS:

"And I say unto you,_____, and it shall be given you; _____, and ye shall find;_____, and it shall be opened unto you"

Think of your favorite T.V. show. It's hard to take your eyes off of it when it's on. Why? Because it's your favorite show! God would love for all of us to have that same attention when seeking Him in His word or in prayer, Amen.

Grandpa Morris

MORRIS

WYDE

72

47 MANNA VILLE'S RETIREMENT VILLAGE

PLAYING CARDS WITH HIS NEIGHBORS AT THE RETIREMENT HOME, AND VISITING FAMILY OVER THE WEEKENDS.

TRING TO STAY YOUTHFUL AS MUCH AS POSSIBLE WITHOUT BREAKING ANY OF HIS ELDERLY LIMBS!

Rufus and Clyde and The Stench of Doom

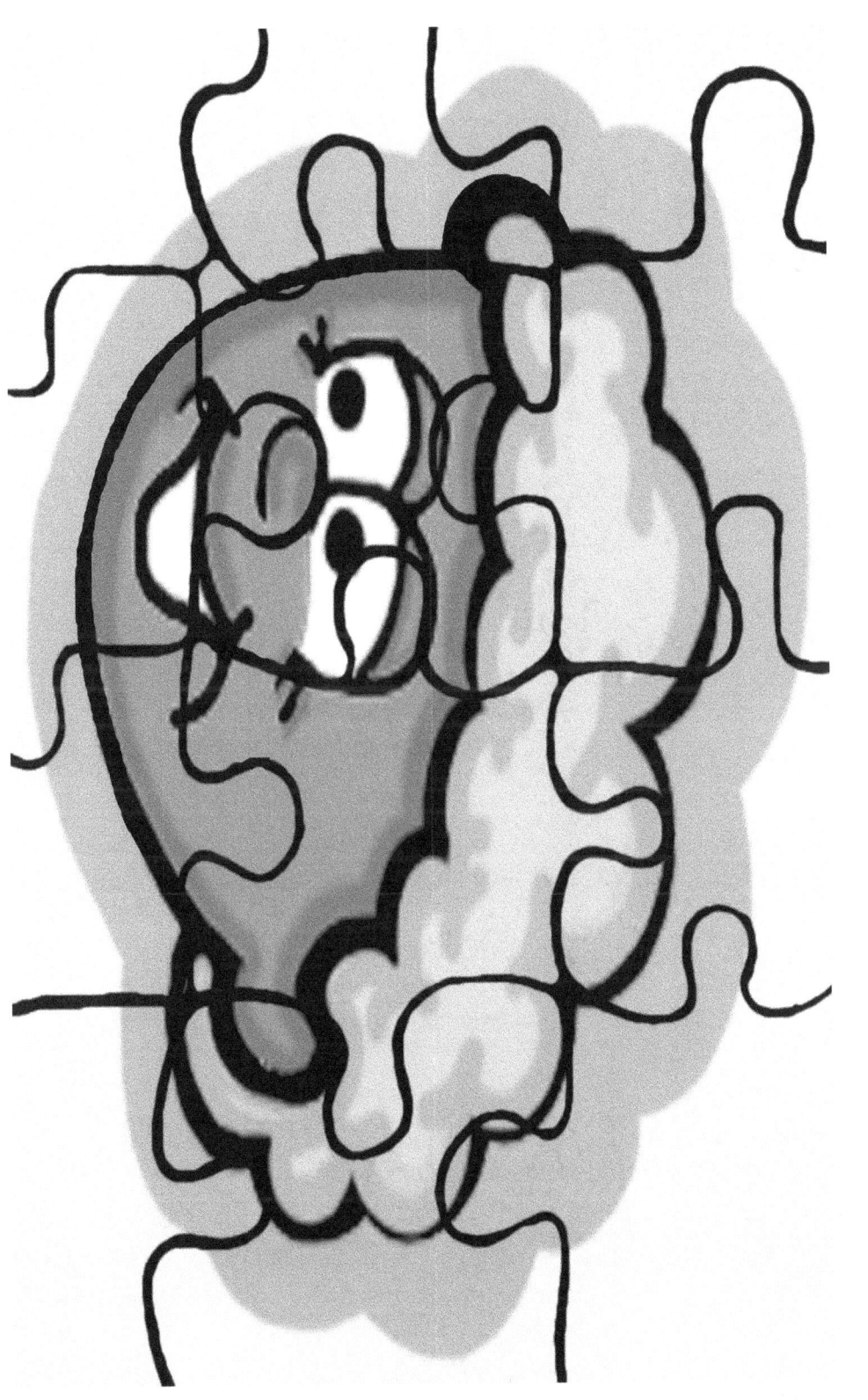

HoneyKeep Ministries
HoneyKeep Ministries
HoneyKeep Minis
HoneyKeep Ministries
HoneyKeep Minis
HoneyKeep Ministries

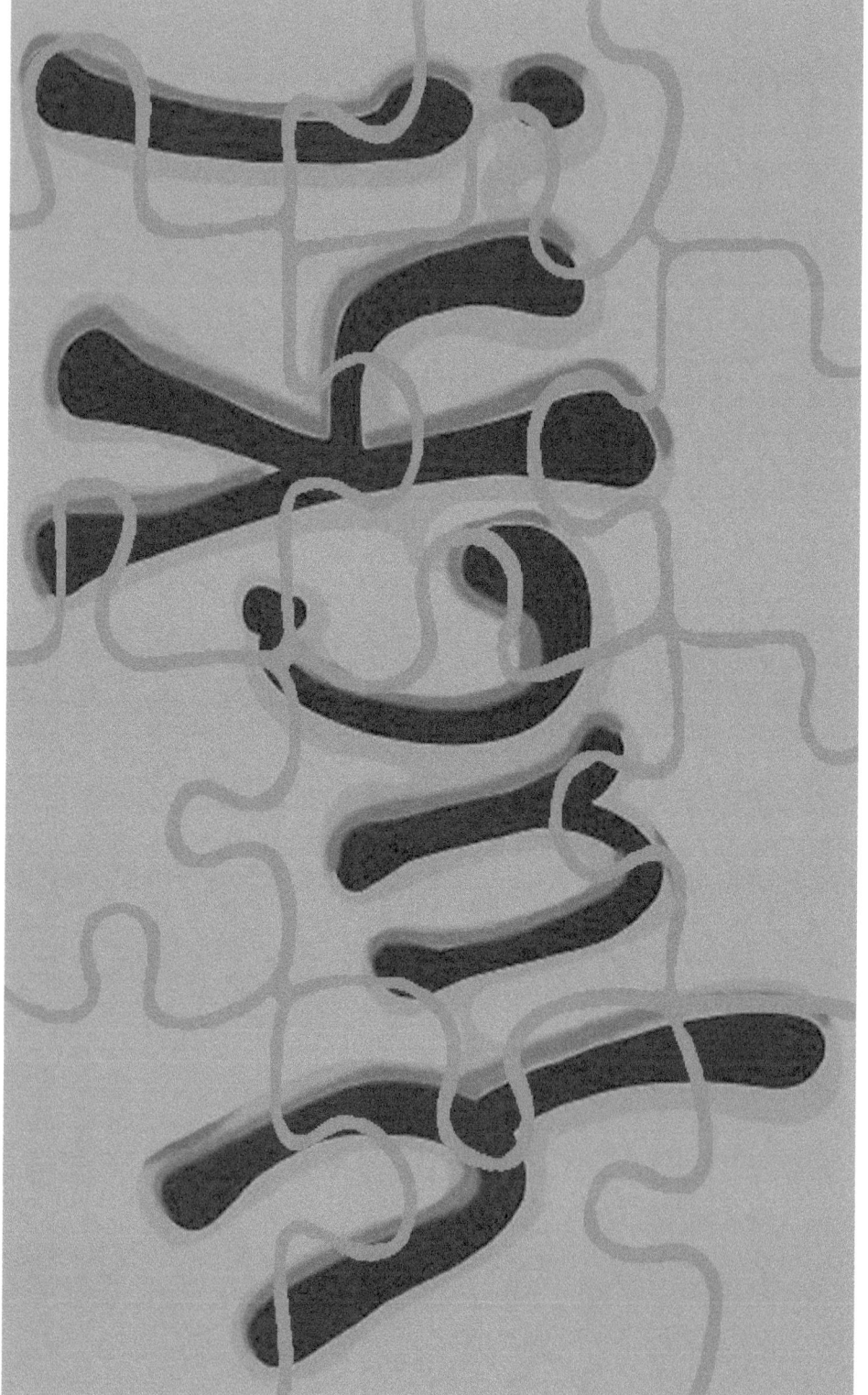

Day 32

Read (LUKE 11:10) KJV and fill in the missing words:

"For everyone who_____receiveth; and that_____findeth;
and to him that_____it shall be opened"

Try to imagine the largest and biggest thing that you can. Now think of some place to hide it. If what you thought of was big enough, it would be hard to hide. Did you know that God is even bigger and stronger than that! So when we pray and seek Him, His ears are large enough to hear us, Amen!

The Wyde Family Fun Facts!

Fact 1: The Wyde's have been living at 42 Sand Street for 11 years!

Fact 2: They are not too popular with the neighbors because of Rufus pranks!

Fact 3: The Wyde family are faith based and believe in going to church every Sunday!

Fact 4: The Wyde's do not own any pets because Rufus is not good at taking care of them. Even when he gets help from his friend Clyde!

Fact 5: The Wyde's idea of family fun is staying home and watching movies together!

Rufus and Clyde and The Stench of Doom

Day 33

..........Grandpa Morris bedroom was on the first floor, not too far from the kitchen. When they arrived at his bedroom door they found it slightly opened, they could see the dancing light flickering through the crack of his door. Thinking he's awake watching TV, they entered the room to talk to him about the stench. But there was no Grandpa Morris. The television was on, but the chair and bed lay empty within the room. Where was Grandpa Morris? The two looked at each other in confusion wondering where such an old man could have gone....................

READ (1 Kings 22: 5) KJV **AND FILL IN THE MISSING WORDS:**

"And Jehoshaphat_____unto the_____of Israel,_____,
I_____thee, at the_____of the_____today"

my special prayer . . . .

WHERE IN THE WORLD IS GRANDPA MORRIS?
IT LOOKS LIKE WHAT'S CAUSING THIS STENCH ISN'T THE ONLY THING THAT'S HARD TO FIND.
BUT DON'T FEAR, THINGS CAN EASILY BE FOUND IF YOU JUST ASK GOD IN PRAYER.
WHAT'S YOUR PRAYER REQUEST TODAY?

_____
_____
_____
_____
_____
_____
_____
_____
_____
_____

In your name I pray, Amen.

Rufus and Clyde and The Stench of Doom

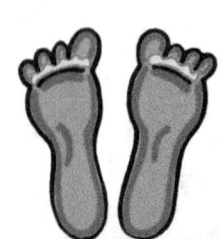

Read (Psalm 119:10) KJV

In the story of Solomon in the bible (2 Chronicles 1:7-12), God asked Solomon what is it that He desired? When Solomon answered, God rewarded him with what he asked for and so much more. God desires us to come to Him for everything, He will supply us with more than we could ever ask or think!

Reading Challenge Today: Let's see if you can read yesterday's story UPSIDE DOWN!

....

Grandpa Morris bedroom was on the first floor, not too far from the kitchen. When they arrived at his bedroom door they found it slightly opened, they could see the dancing light flickering through the crack of his door. Thinking he's awake watching TV, they entered the room to talk to him about the stench. But there was no Grandpa Morris. The television was on, but the chair and bed lay empty within the room. Where was Grandpa Morris? The two looked at each other in confusion wondering where such an old man could have gone.............

Rufus and Clyde and The Stench of Doom

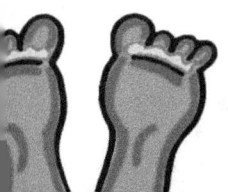 you get a star!!!

Read (Job 11:7) KJV

"Canst thou by searching **find** out God? canst thou find out the Almighty unto perfection?"

PEOPLE ARE OFTEN AFRAID TO ASK A QUESTION FROM TIME TO TIME. ESPECIALLY IF WE FEEL OUR QUESTION IS SILLY OR DUMB. GOD HOWEVER WILL NEVER LOOK AT US STRANGE OR TREAT US AS THOUGH WE ARE SILLY FOR ASKING A QUESTION. WE SHOULD ALL THANK OUR GOD FOR THAT, AMEN!

Here are some clues for tomorrows story:

Smells   Grandpa Morris   Flush

Stink

So what do you think of the clues for tomorrow's story, think you can figure out what will happen?
Seek out some ideas while playing Memory Cards from Day 6!

**1. Mix them up   2. Place them face down
3. Match all the cards that are alike**

Rufus and Clyde and The Stench of Doom

……......Then they heard a sound, it was the sound of a toilet flushing and running water. Grandpa
Morris was just in the bathroom to their relief. So they walked over towards the bathroom just in
time as he began to open the door. Grandpa Morris came out with his cane and greeted them with a
laugh.

"Boys what are you still doing up? Are you having an adventure?" And just before they could answer the question, another smell began to feel their nostrils. They quickly forgot about the previous lingering odor and focused hard on the present stench coming from the bathroom. Grandpa Morris ate something that did not agree with him nor anyone else. This was a horrible stench!...................

Read (ROMANS 2: 7) KJV

Poor Rufus and Clyde, will their noses ever have relief from smelly odors?
Grandpa Morris isn't helpful at all!
Putting away BAD smells, let's focus on the GOOD things Christ can stand for in our lives. Circle ALL the positive things Christ means to you below:

Tissue	Friend	Tooth Brush
Peace	Shower Curtain	Good Listener
Towels	Bathroom	Flush
Protector	Happiness	Handle
Wash Cloth	Soap	Kindness
Teacher	Cleaner	Mirror
Air Freshener	Joy	Father
Strengh	Tub	Cabinet
Bath Mat	Healer	Love

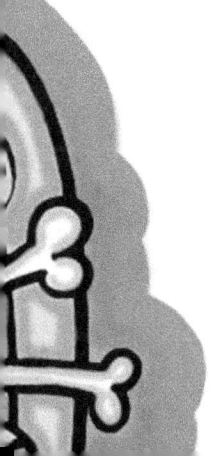

Rufus and Clyde and The Stench of Doom

Day 37

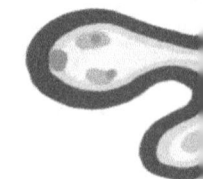

Read (EZRA 8:23) KJV and fill in the missing words:

"So_____fasted and besought our God for this:_____he was intreated of us"

Can a person ask too many questions? Sure if asked at the wrong time. For instance, asking Grandpa Morris about his bathroom odor is a bad idea. Don't ask Rufus and Clyde! But lucky for us, our God is never embarrassed by our silly questions. And He's never too busy to answer the questions asked at the wrong time.

NOW LET'S TEST YOU ON WHAT YOU REMEMBER FROM YESTERDAY'S STORY:

What question did Grandpa Morris ask Rufus and Clyde when he seen them?

A. Are you having an adventure?
B. Do you both need to use the bathroom?
C. What time is it?
D. Can you help me back to my room?

What sound did Rufus and Clyde hear when they were looking for Grandpa Morris?

A. Music & singing
B. Toilet flushing & running water
C. Shower running
D. Brushing teeth

Who was responsible for the new odor Rufus and Clyde began to smell?

A. Rufus
B. Clyde
C. Mrs Wyde
D. Grandpa Morris

What does Grandpa Morris use to help him walk better?

A. A walker
B. A wheelchair
C. A cane
D. A crutch

Awesome!!

Rufus and Clyde and The Stench of Doom

Day 38

Read (1 CHRONICLES 16:11) KJV and fill in the missing words:

"_____the LORD and his_____, seek his face continually"

Sometimes asking a question can be scary, especially if we're fearful of the answer. One thing is for sure about Christ, whatever answer He may give, He always knows what is best for us, Amen!

◀ Can you draw Grandpa Morris?

Rufus and Clyde and The Stench of Doom

Day 39

………..What's the matter, cat got your tongue?

Grandpa Morris could see them struggling as they stood there speechless attempting not to inhale the ghastly odor in. Offended by their reaction, Grandpa Morris decided to cut their visit short. "You think that's something" he said as he pointed towards the bathroom door. "That's nothing compared to that stinking odor that's been plaguing this house for the last hour"………….

READ (Proverbs 28: 5) KJV **AND FILL IN ALL THE MISSING WORDS:**

"_____men   understand_____judgement: but_____
        that_____the_____understand_____things"

So Grandpa Morris is not the cause of both odors.
Then who is? I guess Rufus and Clyde are going to have to keep searching.
While they search, take the time to connect the Biblical things and persons that go together:

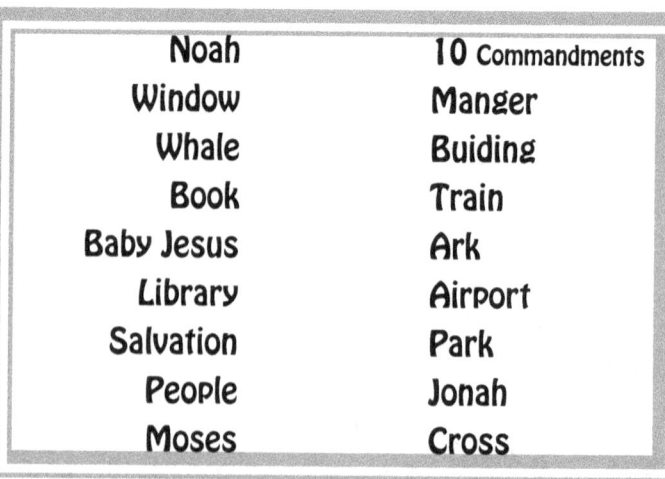

Noah	10 Commandments
Window	Manger
Whale	Buiding
Book	Train
Baby Jesus	Ark
Library	Airport
Salvation	Park
People	Jonah
Moses	Cross

Rufus and Clyde and The Stench of Doom

Read (Deuteronomy 12:5) KJV

..........."What's the matter, cat got your tongue?

Yuck!

Grandpa Morris could see them struggling as they stood there

Speechless attemping not to inhale the ghastly odor in.

Yuck!

Offended by their reactions, Grandpa Morris decided to

cut their visit short. "You think that's something"

Yuck!

he said as he pointed towards the bathroom door. "That's nothing compared to that stinking odor

Yuck!

that's been plaguing the house........

Ewww! Can someone pass Grandpa Morris the air freshener? Have you ever asked for something you really wanted? Of course you're hoping the answer is "yes". It fills us with joy when we get what we desire. God also desires us to pray and ask Him some questions as well. And just like our loved ones, He wants us to be happy and fulfilled.

TRY AND SEE IF YOU CAN READ YESTERDAY'S STORY "MAZE STYLE!"

Rufus and Clyde and The Stench of 1

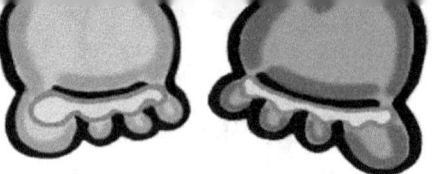

PLAY CARDS! Day 41

(John 10:9) "I am the door: by me if any man enter in, he shall be saved, and shall go in and out, and find pasture"

Sometimes we're impatient waiting on an answer to a question we've asked. Waiting can be difficult at times, but worth it. We need to give God all the time He needs, so things will work out in our favor.

Here are some clues to tomorrows story:

So what do you think of the clues for tomorrow's story, think you can figure out what will happen? Seek out some ideas while playing Memory Cards from Day 6!

1. Mix them up   2. Place them face down
3. Match all the cards that are alike

Rufus and Clyde and The Stench of Doom

Rufus and Clyde glanced at each other briefly.

"Besides little James made a stink just the other day and I liked to keel over. Shoot, his dirty diapers might be the reason for this odor in this house right now. I don't know what Tonya is feeding that baby for him to make a huge stink like that!" And Grandpa Morris walked passed them, entered his room and closed the door.................

Read (2 CHRONICLES 7: 14) KJV **and fill in the missing words:**

"If my_____, which are called by my_____, shall humble themselves, and_____, and seek my_____, and turn from their_____ways; then will I hear from_____, and will forgive their_____, and will heal their_____"

DIRTY DIAPERS? IS THAT WHAT'S BEHIND THIS FOUL ODOR?

TONYA'S GOT SOME MAJOR EXPLAINING TO DO.

IT LOOKS LIKE THEY'RE CONNECTING THE DOTS AND SOLVING THE MYSTERY. SPEAKING OF CONNECTING THE DOTS; TAKE THE TIME TO CONNECT THE BIBLE PEOPLE WITH THE BOOK OF THE BIBLE THEIR STORY IS FOUND IN:

Diaper	Matthew
Adam and Eve	Bottle
Teething Ring	Samson
John The Baptist	Baby Bag
Pacifier	1 Samuel
Judges	Solomon
Giant Goliath	rattle
Wipes	Genesis
1 Kings	Onesie

Rufus and Clyde and The Stench of

Day 43

Read (Judges 18:5) KJV and fill in the missing words:

"And they said unto him,_____counsel, we pray thee, of God, that we may_____whether our way which we go shall_____ prosperous"

No one enjoys taking out the trash, especially when it smelly like this odor Rufus and Clyde are trying to discover. Unfortunately, chores like this must be done. But did you know that God is never tired or uninterested in doing anything for us. Whatever we ask of Him, He is ready and able to fulfill it. AMEN!

Now let's quiz you on how well you remember yesterday's story:

What is the baby's name mentioned by Grandpa Morris?

A. Jesse
B. John
C. James
D. Little J.

What is the baby's mother name mentioned by Grandpa?

A. Theresa
B. Tonya
C. Tiffany
D. Tara

Why did Grandpa Morris blame the baby?

A. Because his diapers were very smelly
B. Because he cried all day long
C. Because the baby told him
D. Because the baby made a mess

Grandpa Morris went where after talking with Rufus & Clyde?

A. To the kitchen to get a snack
B. To the living room to watch T.V.
C. He left the house and went home
D. Back to his room

Nicely Done!

Rufus and Clyde and The Stench of Doom

Read (Psalm 77:6) KJV

When an answer to our questions don't come fast enough, it can be helpful to take our minds off the problem. Giving God praise for just who He is and thanking Him for the small things should do the trick, Amen!

Can you draw Little James stinky diaper?

Rufus and Clyde and The Stench of Doom

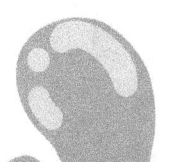

..............Unknown to Grandpa Morris, he answered the very question they failed to ask.

"It stinks over here!" Clyde muffled from behind his hand covering his nose and mouth.

"Yeah it does, let's get out of here" So they headed upstairs towards Tonya's room..................

Read (Acts 17: 27) KJV and fill in the missing words:

"That they should_____the Lord, if haply they might_____ after him, and_____him, though he be not_____from every one_____us"

Have you ever been curious about something and got your answer without asking!
God is ALL KNOWING. He is the GREAT I AM.
Below is a group of things God can be when we need Him, please circle **ALL that apply:**

Aroma	Listener	Savior
Friend	Gas	Father
Perfume	Mildew	Skunk
Scent	Provider	Foul
Deliver	Tang	Whiff
Fragrance	Stench	Skunk
Stink	Comforter	Teacher
Healer	Reek	Smelly
Miracle Worker	Smell	Protector

ıfus and Clyde and The Stench of Doom

Day 46

Read (2 chronicles 20:4) KJV and fill in the missing words:

"And Judah gathered_____together, to ask help of the_____:
even out of all the cities of Judah they_____to seek the LORD"

We ask for directions when we're lost or confused about something. And sometimes the person we may ask might not have the correct answer or no the answer at all. Thank the Lord we have a God that knows all, and always knows the right answer and direction we should go. **Hopefully God gives Rufus and Clyde a direction away from this bad odor!**

Let's see if you can read yesterday's story "Mirror Style":

.............Unknown to Grandpa Morris, he answered the very question they failed to ask.

"It stinks over here!" Clyde muffled from behind his hand covering his nose and mouth.

"Yeah it does, let's get out of here" So they headed upstairs towards Tonya's room...................

Hint: Place backward words above in front of a mirror and watch the words appear normal again!

Terrific!!!

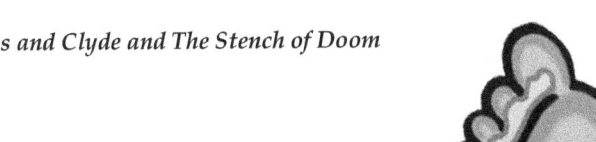
Rufus and Clyde and The Stench of Doom

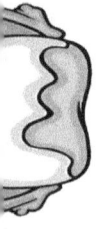

Play Cards!

Day 47

(Luke 15:8) "Either what woman having ten pieces of silver, if she lose one piece, doth not light a candle, and sweep the house, and seek diligently till she *find* it?"

Knocking for a door to be open does not mean people will always allow us to enter in. It could be because they're playing with us or maybe because they're upset. But whenever we knock on heaven's door with prayer, we can be confident that God will open up and let us in each time.

Here are some clues about tomorrow's story:

TONYA AND BABY JAMES   Questions   Sleeping   Blankets

So what do you think of the clues for tomorrow's story, think you can figure out what will happen? Seek out some ideas while playing Memory Cards **from Day 61**

**1. MIX THEM UP 2. PLACE THEM FACE DOWN
3. MATCH ALL THE CARDS THAT ARE ALIKE**

Rufus and Clyde and The Stench of Doom

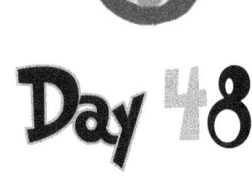

Day 48

............Slowly Rufus opened the door to Tonya's room. Tonya and her infant son James were sleeping soundly. Tonya lay snuggled in her blanket with the remote control barely in her hand soon to hit the floor, and comfortably sandwiched between two stuffed animals was baby James with an empty bottle resting above his head. They appeared to have hit a dead end. There would be no questioning cousin Tonya tonight, unfortunately they would have to wait until tomorrow.....................

Read (JEREMIAH 29: 13) KJV

**Wow, they're both asleep. What are Rufus and Clyde going to do now? I guess we'll find out tomorrow.
In the meantime; they can pray and ask God for help.
Below write down your special prayer to God today:**

MY SPECIAL PRAYER. . . .

In Jesus name I pray, Amen

Rufus and Clyde and The Stench of Doom

Day 49 Yuck!

"Search me, O _____, and know my_____: try me, and_____my thoughts"

Have you ever asked for something and got more than what you asked for? God enjoys answering our prayer's and showering us down with those things we need in our lives. Let's continue to ask God for direction and growth, Amen! And let's also hope that Rufus and Clyde can get some answers in Tonya and baby James room.

Think you remember yesterday's story? Answer these questions and see for yourself!

What was Tonya and baby James doing when Rufus and Clyde came into their room?

A. They were sleeping
B. Tonya was reading to Baby James
C. They were playing
D. Watching T.V.

Why did Rufus and Clyde want to talk to Tonya?

A. They wanted to say goodnight
B. They wanted to play a prank
C. She kept to the corner of the bed and
D. She asked them to come

How is Tonya related to Rufus?

A. She's his mother
B. She's his best friend
C. She's his neighbor
D. She's his cousin

What was Tonya holding in her hands?

A. Tissue
B. T.V. remote control
C. A soiled diaper
D. Nothing

 **Beautifully Done!!**

Rufus and Clyde and The Stench of Doom

Draw a Masterpiece!

READ (ECCLESIASTES 7:25) KJV

Sometimes people can knock on the door and we don't even hear them knocking. Perhaps if they would knock a little louder we would have heard them. One thing is for sure, no matter how hard or soft we knock when we pray to God, he will always hear us.

Can you draw this spit ball?
Try it and see!

Slendid!!

Rufus and Clyde and The Stench of Doom

Day 51

.............."How can they sleep in this stink?" Clyde whispered.

"Maybe they don't smell it"

"Don't smell it, are you crazy?"

"I don't know, c'mon let's get out of here". Just as Rufus was about to close the door suddenly he got a whiff of another unpleasant odor coming from the room. Clyde noticed it soon after and they both quietly entered the room to see what it was. The smell grew stronger and stronger as they made their way closer to the foot of the bed were Tonya laid..................

Read (ISAIAH 55: 6) KJV

WORD SEARCH LIST:

Isaiah
Psalm
Job
Genesis
Esther
Jonah
Hebrews
Jude
Titus
Acts
John
Romans

YUck!!

Something foul is in Tonya and baby James room.
Rufus and Clyde should take their time and search it out.
While they look, take the time and find the books of the bible in the word search below:

I	S	A	I	A	H	T	J	F	H	E	B	I	B
W	L	U	Y	M	F	Y	G	P	R	Q	A	O	L
H	E	B	R	T	W	S	B	R	X	R	J	Z	A
C	J	F	Y	D	M	U	P	D	A	Q	H	F	C
J	O	H	N	C	Y	S	P	H	O	K	L	H	T
N	T	P	G	X	I	E	Y	U	X	G	N	M	S
S	R	G	B	S	U	Y	J	U	D	E	B	R	D
W	J	U	E	U	E	E	C	S	Q	Y	M	F	T
M	B	N	U	D	C	Y	S	C	P	O	U	G	I
E	E	Q	C	Y	J	M	E	T	W	B	Z	O	T
G	W	J	O	N	A	H	D	J	H	B	D	J	U
Q	E	C	Y	J	Z	R	X	C	Y	E	T	B	S
Z	L	R	O	M	A	N	S	G	U	S	R	K	F

Awesome Work!!

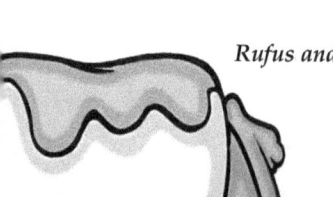

Rufus and Clyde and The Stench of Doom

Day 52

Read (Jeremiah 17:10) KJV and fill in the missing words:

"I the LORD search the_____, I try the reins, even to give every man
according_____his ways, and according to
the_____of his doings"

Let's see if you can read yesterday's story "Circle Style"

suddenly he got a whiff of another unpleasant odor coming from the room. Clyde noticed it soon after and they both quietly entered the room to see what it was... "I don't know, c'mon let's get out of here." Just as Rufus was about to close the door

You're the Best!

Rufus and Clyde and The Stench of Doom

Play Cards!

Day 53

(Luke 15:4) "What man of you, having an hundred sheep, if he lose one of them, doth not leave the ninety and nine in the wilderness, and go after that which is lost, until he **find** it?"

Question, how large do you think heaven's door is? What if the knob is too tall for us to reach? Or the door is too big for us to open up? These are questions that make God appear too BIG and unreachable and untouchable. But this is not so, God is actually in our hearts and we can call on Him in prayer at anytime!

Here are some clues to tomorrow's story:

Another stink

So what do you think of the clues for tomorrow's story? Think you can figure out what will happen?

Waste Basket

Seek out some ideas while playing Memory Cards from Day 6!

Smells

1. Mix them up
2. Place them face down
3. Match all the cards that are alike

Baby James

your a natural!!

Rufus and Clyde and The Stench of Doom

Day 54

To their surprise sat a small waste basket full of foul smelling soiled diapers. Grandpa Morris was right! Cousin Tonya must be feeding the baby something rotten and foul! They both left the room and closed the door. While back in the hallway, they were approached by another stench, the original stench they have been trying to get to the bottom of this whole night.....................

Read (Colossians **: 1-2) KJV and fill in the missing words:**

"If ye then be_____with Christ,_____those things which are above, where_____sitteth on the right_____of God. Set your affection on things_____, not on things on the_____"

Stinky diapers, smelly bathrooms, bad food, the list just goes on and on.

Don't give up Rufus and Clyde, God is always on time.
Being **encouraged** that God can work things out if we **trust** and have **patience** is hard work!
Now try working hard describing what these three things mean to you:

TRUST in God means to me......	**patience** in God means to me....

Okay!

Being ENCOURAGED means to me:

Rufus and Clyde and The Stench of Doom

Day 55

Read (John 5:39) KJV and fill in the missing words:

"Search the_____; for in them ye think ye_____eternal
life: and they are_____which testify of me"

There are times when we may not be excited letting someone in when they knock on our door. Sometimes people are destructive and do not respect the things we may have. Just know that letting God into the door of our heart will never be a mistake. God loves us, respect us and will never let us down.

Now let's see how well you remember yesterday's story:

What was the waste basket full of in Tonya and baby James room?

A. Spoiled food
B. Dirty laundry
C. Smelly diapers
D. Perfume

What size was the waste basket in Tonya and Baby James room?

A. Hugh
B. Small
C. Large
D. Medium

Rufus and Clyde noticed what returning back in the hallway?

A. T.V. in the living room was on
B. Everyone was asleep
C. The smell was gone
D. The odor was still there

Who did Rufus and Clyde think was right about Tonya and baby James causing the stink?

A. Grandpa Morris
B. Mr. Wyde
C. Mrs. Wyde
D. Aliens from space

GOLDEN!!

Rufus and Clyde and The Stench of Doom

Read (PSALM 139:1) KJV

Have you ever sold candy bars going door-to-door? If you have, then you know to greet potential buyers with a smile and try to sell as many as you can, HA HA! But did you know that God is twice as sweet as any candy bar we have ever tasted? And He desires that we knock on His door with prayer so He can reward us with a tasty treat, Amen!

Pure perfection!

Can you draw your own stinky slime? Give it a try!

Rufus and Clyde and The Stench of Doom

Day 57

"Well that's a downer". Clyde said in disappointment once he realized the diaper stench was not the same stench in the hallway.

Rufus leaned against the wall and sighed deeply "I know".

Getting down to this stench has left them frustrated, tired and bummed out. So they decided to throw in the towel, and suffer in silence for the rest of the night. Morning would hopefully shed some light on the stench and breathing would be enjoyable again. As they walked towards Rufus's room, they passed the hallway stairs. Standing at the foot of the stairs was Rufus's dad Mr. Wyde. He heard the sound of footsteps walking and decided to sneak a peek to see who it was...........................

Tomorrow morning will hopefully shed more light on their mystery stench.

They can better plan on how they're going to handle it as well.

Take the time now and fill out the "Daily Planner" to the right and plan out this Godly day for yourself:

Read (PSALMS 63: 1) KJV

My Daily Planner:

Morning:	Evening:	Night:
1.	1.	1.
2.	2.	2.
3.	3.	3.
4.	4.	4.
5.	5.	5.
6.	6.	6.

perfect!

Rufus and Clyde and The Stench of Doom

Day 58

Read (ACTS 17:11) KJV and fill in the missing words:

"_____were more noble than those in Thessalonica, in that_____ received the word all readiness of mind,_____searched the scriptures daily, whether those_____were so"

There are many ways to get someone to open the door without knocking. You can call them by phone, ring the doorbell or simply call their name.

It is the same with God; we can get God's attention by praying, reading the bible, going to church and even being active in the church. God will see it all, and will gladly open His door of blessings, Amen.

See if you can read yesterday's story "Upside Down" style:

"Well that's a downer", Clyde said in disappointment once he realized the diaper stench was not the same stench in the hallway.

Rufus leaned against the wall and sighed deeply "I know".

Getting down to this stench has left them frustrated, tired and bummed out. So they decided to throw in the towel, and suffer in silence for the rest of the night. Morning would hopefully shed some light on the stench and breathing would be enjoyable again. As they walked towards Rufus's room, they passed the hallway stairs. Standing at the foot of the stairs was Rufus's dad Mr. Wyde. He heard the sound of footsteps walking and decided to sneak a peek to see who it was...........

Perfection!!

Draw a picture! Day 59

Read (1 Peter 1:10) KJV

During an emergency (like this stinky odor, Yikes!), we can knock on a door pretty hard to get someone's attention. We need help right away and want someone to answer fast.

During emergencies, always remember to also pray and knock on God's door as well.

He'll help us get through all scary and important situations.

Can you draw bones? Give it a try and see for yourself!

Rufus and Clyde and The Stench of Doom

Delightful!!

Day 60

"SEEKING GOD"

Read (Proverbs 8:17) KJV

"I love them that love me; and those that seek me early shall find me" (Proverbs 8: 17). There it is in a nut shell, beautifully put in this verse from the bible about how God enjoys our worship time with Him. He wants us to find the time during the day to say "I love you". Just think about it. We all desire to be noticed and appreciated, nobody likes being ignored or rejected. Let's ALL give God His quality time that He deserves.

Rufus and Clyde and The Stench of Doom

Day 61

Read (Revelation 3:20) **KJV and fill in the missing words:**

"Behold, I stand at the_____r, and knock: if any man hear my_____, and open the door, I will come in to him, and_____sup with him, and_____with me"

Ha Have you ever opened the door for someone you thought was somebody else? Mistakes will happen, but a mistake like this can be very dangerous. God however doesn't make mistakes like this, it's because He is everywhere and anywhere! He's always aware of who's knocking on His door at ALL times, Amen!

The Palms Family Fun Facts!

Fact 1:	The Palms have been living at 90 Cactus Road for 16 years!
Fact 2:	The Palms love animals, and Clyde's father is a shepherd!
Fact 3:	The Palms are very active in their church!
Fact 4:	Mrs. Palms and Mrs. Wyde are really good friends!
Fact 5:	The Palms idea of family fun is going on a road trip or camping!

What Fun!!

Rufus and Clyde and The Stench of Doom

HoneyKeep Ministri

yKeep Ministries

HoneyKeep Ministri

eyKeep Ministries

HoneyKeep Ministri

yKeep Ministries

READ (Jeremiah 6:16) KJV AND FILL IN THE MISSING WORDS:

"Thus saith the LORD, _____ye in the ways, and see, and ask for the old_____, where is the_____way, and walk therein, and ye shall find_____for your souls. But they said, We will not walk therein"

We all know what it's like waiting on someone. Especially going somewhere fun and exciting, we'll wait at the door while peeking out the window every few minutes.

God gets just as excited when we get on our knees to pray or study His word. He can't wait for that time of fellowship with us.

Baby James Fun Facts!

First Name:	James
Last Name:	Wyde
Age:	7 months
Address:	42 Sands Street in Manna's Ville
Hobbies:	Sucking thumb, playing, discovering new things to taste and chewing on toys!
Goals:	Interested in learning how to walk soon so he can get into more trouble!

Be Blessed!!!

Rufus and Clyde and The Stench of Doom

"Ya'll not in bed yet". He replied surprisingly while pouring some potato chips into a bowl.

"Why don't you both join me in watching an old movie, that'll surely put you to sleep!" Rufus and Clyde headed back down the stairs without any interest in asking about the stench. They've truly given up on the matter. Mr. Wyde fixed some snacks while going on and on about his hard day at work. His constant chatter went unnoticed though, they were too tired out. After grabbing enough snacks to go around, they left the kitchen and sat on the couch. Mr. Wyde grabbed the remote and hit the play button for the movie to start.....................

READ (1 Chronicles 16: 10) KJV

Not a peep out of Rufus and Clyde about the stench, they've really given up! Let's not be like Rufus and Clyde and keep our mouths shut. Let's make our requests known to God in prayer today. Amen! Write down your special prayer below:

My Special Prayer . . . . . .

Thank you Father, Amen.

Rufus and Clyde and The Stench of Doom

Olympic Reading Challenge:

Day 64

Read John 7:34 KJV

Question, how do we know when God is knocking on the door of our hearts? Let's think about it. Do we want people to notice us, talk to us, love us and appreciate us?
Well so does God, so lets share this day with Him, with praying and reading the word, Amen!

LET'S SEE HOW WELL YOU CAN READ A SAMPLE OF YESTERDAY'S STORY "MAZE STYLE":

"Ya'll not in bed yet". He said surprisingly as he poured potato chips into a bowl. "Why don't you both join me in watching an old movie, that'll surely put you to sleep!" Rufus and Clyde headed back down the stairs w*ithout any interest in asking what he knew about the stench. They truly gave up on the mat-ter Mr. Wyde fixed some late night snacks while going on about his hard day...

Rufus and Clyde and The Stench of Doom

Day 65

(Luke 12:37) "Blessed are those servants, whom the lord when he cometh shall *FIND* watching: verily I say unto you, that he shall gird himself, and make them to sit down to meat, and will come forth and serve them"

Corny Knock Knock Jokes!

Knock Knock!   Who's there?
God is Wow   God is Wow who?
God is Wow – derful! HA HA!!
God is a Wonderful Savior!

Here are some clues to tomorrow's story:

Fun   Forgot   WATCH T.U.   ODOR

So what do you think of the clues for tomorrow's story, think you can figure out what will happen?
Seek out some ideas while playing Memory Cards from Day 6!

**1. Mix them up   2. Place them face down
3. Match all the cards that are alike**

Sweet!!

Rufus and Clyde and The Stench of Doom

Day 66

…………Laughter and enjoyment soon filled the room, and overtime Rufus and Clyde forgot all about the odor. They were having too much fun. The stench wasn't so bothersome once they took their minds off of it. Perhaps it was never a big issue in the first place. Finally the boys were having a pleasant night again……………

Read **(Zephaniah 2: 3) KJV** and fill in the missing words:

"Seek ye the Lord, all ye_____of the earth, which_____wrought his judgement; seek_____, seek_____: it may be ye shall be_____in the day of the_____anger"

One of the fruits of the spirit is peace. Take the time now and search for the many fruits of the spirit:

Word search List:

P	I	M	E	E	K	N	E	S	S	L	M	G	W
U	E	H	Q	R	B	U	W	G	O	Y	N	R	L
E	Q	A	H	R	D	C	S	R	R	I	E	N	P
L	W	H	C	Z	X	D	T	P	R	S	K	T	A
O	T	Y	U	E	C	N	K	E	Z	H	I	U	T
U	S	L	N	R	O	J	F	O	J	T	N	E	I
E	X	Q	E	C	H	F	C	R	O	W	D	J	E
J	R	K	F	T	U	K	Z	D	Y	T	N	E	N
Y	Q	L	F	S	F	E	S	B	U	L	E	T	C
A	E	B	G	Y	F	R	U	I	T	H	S	R	E
S	Z	N	X	B	Y	R	K	I	E	K	S	Y	Q
Y	O	M	Y	G	E	N	T	L	E	N	E	S	S
L	R	U	J	F	S	X	N	G	U	S	F	U	L

GENTLENESS
PATIENCE
LOVE
LONG SUFFERING
FRUIT
KINDNESS
PEACE
LONG SUFFERING
JOY
MEEKNESS

Rufus and Clyde and The Stench of I

Read **[NUMBERS 10:33] KJV** and fill in the missing words:

"And they departed_____the mount of the LORD three days' journey:
and_____ark of the covenant of the LORD went before_____
in the three days' journey, to_____out a resting place for them"

CORNY KNOCK KNOCK JOKES!

"Knock. Knock!"   "Who's there?"
"Sal"   "Sal who?"
"Sal - vation!" HA HA!
Jesus is the God of our Salvation!

LET'S SEE HOW MUCH YOU REMEMBER ABOUT YESTERDAY'S STORY:

What was Rufus and Clyde doing with Mr. Wyde?

A. Eating and watching a movie
B. Playing video games
C. Talkng about school and grades
D. Helping clean up

What did Rufus and Clyde almost forget about?

A. What they ate for dinner
B. Going to bed
C. Talking to Tonya
D. The stinky odor

(True or False) Was this sentence in yesterday's story:
"They were having too much fun!"

A. True
B. False

(Yes or No) Was this sentence in yesterday's story:
"They made the problem bigger by focusing on it"

A. Yes
B. No

Great Work!!

Rufus and Clyde and The Stench of Doom

Day 68

Read (1 Peter 1:11) KJV

CORNY KNOCK KNOCK JOKES!

"Knock Knock!"   "Who's there?"
"Hal"   "Hal who?"
"Hal - lellujah" HA HA!!
"Hallellujah, Glory to the Highest!!

Can you draw this
"Yuck" sign?
Go for it!

Yuck!

Brillant!!

Rufus and Clyde and The Stench of Doom

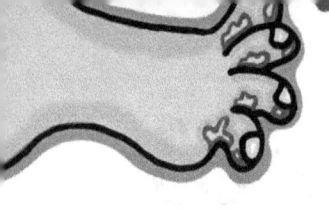

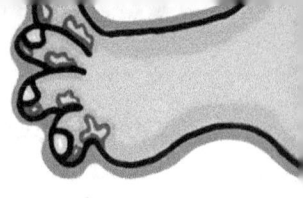

Day 69

…………Mr. Wyde decided to get a little more comfortable by removing his shoes and resting his feet on top of the coffee table. Immediately after removing his shoes, the familiar stench that has been plaguing the entire house returned with the vengeance! IT WAS THE STENCH!! Living inside of Mr. Wyde shoes all along, and sitting up close and personal under Rufus and Clyde's nostrils. The earlier odor smelled like roses compared to this one. Both of them quickly got up and ran off to Mr. Wyde's surprise.

"Hey I thought we were watching the movie?"

"Good night Dad!"

"Yeah good night Mr. Wyde, smell you, I mean see you tomorrow!"………………

SUCCESS!!
AND IT SMELLS
BADD!!
THE MYSTERY
STENCH HAS BEEN
DISCOVERED!
TAKE THE TIME
AND
DISCOVER ALL
THE BOOKS OF
THE BIBLE TO THE
RIGHT AND LEAVE
THE REST.

Job **well Done**

Read (PSALMS 14: 2) KJV

Abraham	Lot	Jonah
Jude	St. John	Goliath
David	Samson	Rachel
Gideon	Micah	Noah
Leah	Stephen	Amos
Saul	Esther	Elijah
Titus	Isaac	Mary
Elisha	Solomon	Joseph
Esau	Jacob	Luke
Ruth	Jesse	Judas

1d Clyde and The Stench of Doom

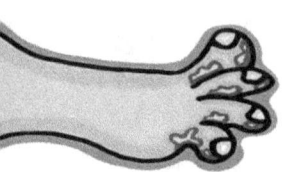

Read (Ezra 8:22) KJV

Corny Knock Knock Jokes!

"Knock Knock!"   **"Who's there?"**
"Tes"   **"Tes who?"**
"Tes - timony!" HA HA!!

God has given us ALL a story to tell about Him, that is our Testimony!

Let's see if you can read yesterday's story "Mirror Style":

.......Mr. Wyde decided to get a little more comfortable by removing his shoes and resting his feet on top of the coffee table. Immediately after removing his shoes, the familiar stench that has been plaguing the entire house returned with the vengeance! IT WAS THE STENCH!! Living inside of Mr. Wyde shoes all along, and sitting up close and personal under Rufus and Clyde's nostrils. The earlier odor smelled like roses compared to this one. Both of them quickly got up and ran off to Mr. Wyde's surprise.

"Hey I thought we were watching the movie?"

"Good night Dad!"

"Yeah good night Mr. Wyde, smell you, I mean see you tomorrow!".....................

Hint: Place backward words above in front of a mirror and watch the words appear normal!

VERY SPECIAL!!

Rufus and Clyde and The Stench of Doom

Play Cards!! Day 7

(Matthew 16:25) "For whosoever will save his life shall lose it: and whosoever will lose his life for my sake shall **find** it"

 Feet

 SMELLY

ODOR

 Tell

MRS. WYDE

CORNY KNOCK KNOCK JOKES!

"Knock Knock!" "Who's there?"
"Al"   "Al who?"
"Al - pha" HA HA!!
God is the beginning (Alpha) of everything!!

Thank God Rufus and Clyde discovered Mr. Wyde's stinky feet! Now try to figure out what they're going to do in tomorrow's story with these clues:

So what do you think of the clues for tomorrow's story, think you can figure out what will happen? Seek out some ideas while playing **Memory Cards** from **Day 6**!

**1. Mix them up   2. Place them face down
3. Match all the cards that are alike**

Rufus and Clyde and The Stench of Doom

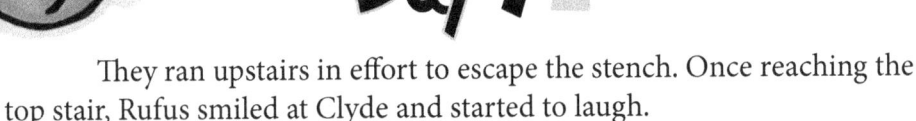

They ran upstairs in effort to escape the stench. Once reaching the top stair, Rufus smiled at Clyde and started to laugh.

"What's so funny?"

"We did it Clyde, we found out what was so smelly here in the house!"

"Oh yeah" Clyde replied with a smile in his voice. "Too bad it's your father's feet though".

"Yeah, that sucks, now how do we fix it?" They both paused and thought about a possible solution for this smelly problem. Neither one of them wanted to tell Mr. Wyde to wash his feet and put his shoes out for garbage. Then Rufus had an idea.

"We'll get my mom to do it for us"

"Good idea"...................

Read (Luke 12: 31) KJV

SMART MOVE RUFUS AND CLYDE, NOW IT'S TIME TO FOCUS ON GETTING RID OF THE STENCH!!! VICTORY IS ONE OF THE BEST FEELINGS IN THE WORLD, ESPECIALLY WHEN IT'S GODLY GIVEN. DESCRIBE BELOW WHAT THESE THREE VICTORIOUS TOPICS IN CHRIST MEANS TO YOU:

Godly Blessings means to me.........

_____

_____

_____

Victory in Christ means to me.........

_____

_____

_____

Godly Miracles means to me........

_____

_____

_____

Alright!

Rufus and Clyde and The Stench of Doom

Day 73

Read (Psalm 77:2) **KJV** and fill in the missing words:

"In the day of my_____I sought the Lord: my sore ran in the _____, and ceased not: my soul refused to_____comforted"

CORNY KNOCK KNOCK JOKES!

"Knock Knock!"   "Who's there?"
"O"   "O who?"
"O - mega" HA HA!!
God is the beginning (Alpha) and the ending (Omega) of ALL things!!

Let's see how much you remember from yesterday's story:

What did Rufus and Clyde discover?

**A. Dirty socks   B. Hidden candy   C. Mr. Wyde's smelly feet
D. More of Baby James diapers**

(True or False)   "Mrs. Wyde food was the cause of the horrible smell!"

A. True   B. False

Who did Rufus think about to tell his father about his feet?

A. His mom   B. Grandpa Morris   C. Tonya   D. His friend Clyde

(Yes or No) **Was this sentence in yesterday's story:**
"We'll get my mom to do it for us"

A. Yes   B. No

Keep up the GOOD Work!!

Rufus and Clyde and The Stench of Doom

Read (Psalm 119:94) KJV

CORNY KNOCK KNOCK JOKES!

"Knock Knock!"   "Who's there?"
"Re"   "Re who?"
"Re - demption" HA HA!!
God has redeemed us and made us whole!!

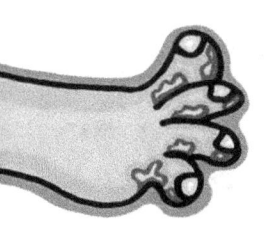

Can you draw this
stinky foot,
PEE EEW!

Rufus and Clyde and The Stench of Doom

incredible!!

Day 75

..........They soon approached Rufus parent's room. The door was closed. Rufus placed his ear to the door for a few seconds listening carefully. "I don't hear anything; I don't think my mom is up".

"We've got to do something, we just can't stand here". They stood in silence pondering their next move. Moments later; Rufus began to softly knock on his parent's door. But still there was no answer.

"We've got to knock harder". Rufus looked at Clyde and nodded in agreement. They both began to knock on the door, and with each fail attempt their knocking grew louder and louder until the knob on the outside began to turn. Mrs. Wyde opened the door in panic thinking something was wrong!................

KNOCK KNOCK! Open the door, Rufus and Clyde's nose depends on it!!!!! God Desires us to seek His face and knock on heaven's door for ALL things. We must remember WHO we are serving. Below match up the people of the bible and things they've done.

Read:

(PSALMS 69: 32)

KJV

Rufus	Gave birth to Jesus
Jesus Christ	Helped solve mystery
Tonya	Baptized Jesus in water
Sarai	Asked family questions
Baby James	Made a stink in diaper
Jonah	Died on the cross
Grandpa Morris	Made bathroom stinky
Mary	Gave birth at old age
Clyde	Mother of baby James
John the Baptist	Swallowed by whale

Rufus and Clyde and The Stench of Doom

Read (Luke 6:19) KJV and fill in the missing words:

"And the_____multitude sought to touch him: for_____
went virtue out of him, and_____them all"

CORNY KNOCK KNOCK JOKES!

"Knock Knock!"   "Who's there?"
"Sam"   "Sam who?"

"Sam – son HA HA!!"

Samson was a mighty warrior used by God and the strongest man to ever live.
(you can read about him in the book of Judges).

Here's a bit of yesterday's story, try and read it "Circle Style":

The door was closed and not a sound was heard from the inside of the bedroom. They realized the possibility that she may be sleeping, but the situation... They approached Rufus parent's bedroom door across from cousin Tonya's.

Rufus and Clyde and The Stench of Doom

Play Cards!!

Day 77

(Matthew 11:29) "Take my yoke upon you, and learn of me; for I am meek and lowly in heart: and ye shall **find** rest unto your souls"

Corny Knock Knock Jokes!

"Knock Knock!"   "Who's there?"
"Eli"   "Eli who?"
"Eli - jah" HA HA!!

Elijah was a prophet used by God in the Old Testament, (you can read about him in the books of 1 Kings & 2 Kings).

Here are some clues to tomorrow's story:

mystery stench   ƎꓷYW ˙SꓤW   Throw away   STINKY SHOES

So what do you think of the clues for tomorrow's story, think you can figure out what will happen? Seek out some ideas while playing Memory Cards from **Day 6!**

1. Mix them up **2.** Place them face down
3. Match all the cards that are alike

OKAY!!

Rufus and Clyde and The Stench of Doom

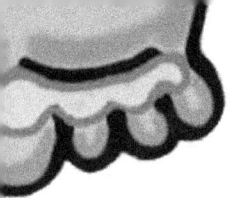
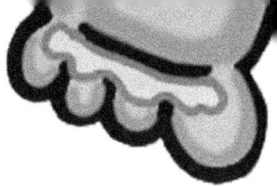

...........But before Mrs. Wyde could ask what was wrong, she was bum rushed by Rufus and Clyde entering the room and talking nonstop about their night. She could barely get a word in.

"Boys alright, one at a time please!"

"We discovered the smell!

"It's Mr. Wyde!"

"Can you tell dad to take a bath?" Mrs. Wyde rolled her eyes and sighed, she was suspicious that her husband may be the problem. She tried to get her husband to throw his old smelly work shoes away for quite some time.

"Don't worry guys, I'll take care of everything" She placed her arms around them both and walked them back to Rufus room to get some sleep...............

READ (Psalms 34: 4) KJV

Whew; thank goodness Mrs. Wyde is planning on telling Mr. Wyde about his smelly feet. Speaking of a plan, what's on your **To Do List Today?** Take the time out below and fill out your "To Do List":

MORNING

1.

2.

3.

4.

5.

6.

EVENING

1.

2.

3.

4.

5.

6.

Have a great Day!

Rufus and Clyde and The Stench of Doom

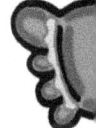

Day 79

Read LUKE 5:18 KJV and fill in the missing words:

"And, behold, men brought in a_____a man which was taken with a palsy: and_____sought means to bring him in, and to_____ him before him"

CORNY KNOCK KNOCK JOKES!

"Knock Knock!"   "Who's there?"
"Je"   "Je who?"
"Je - sus" HA HA!!

Jesus is our Lord and Savior! And because He is One with God, His story is throughout the entire bible.

Quiz time! Lets see how much you remember about yesterday's story:

Where did Mrs. Wyde walk the boys to get some sleep?

A. To Clyde's house
B. Rufus bedroom
C. The tree house
D. To Baby James crib

(True or False) Mrs. Wyde has tried to get Mr. Wyde to throw away his shoes!"

A. True
B. False

(Yes or No) Was this sentence in yesterday's story:
"They were relieved."

A. Yes
B. No

(True or False) Mrs. Wyde assured the boys that she would take care of the problem."

A. True
B. False

YOU GET AN "A" PLUS!!

Rufus and Clyde and The Stench of Doom

Day 80

Read (Luke 4:42) KJV

Corny Knock Knock Jokes!

"Knock Knock!"   "Who's there?"
"O"   "O who?"
"O – prah HA HA!!"

Oprah was the mother-in-law of Ruth, who was a mighty women of God!
(You can find Oprah and Ruth's story in the book of Ruth).

Can you draw
Mrs. Wyde?
Try it and see:

You're a GREAT artist!

Rufus and Clyde and The Stench of Doom

Day 81
Read (Psalms 1: 2) KJV

..........While walking the boys back to the room, she thought that this would be a good time to explain the true reason she encouraged their smelly quest of discovery.

"So you two think the "Ask, seek and knock" scripture sounds like playing hide and seek and telling knock knock jokes, right?

"Umm, that sounds about right mom"

"That's not quite right you two. The asking part is like having a question for God, so you ask in prayer. Sort of like how you both questioned people in the house about the smell. The seeking part is the effort we put into getting our answers by searching and reading our bible. Like how both of you searched every room for that smell without giving up. And finally; praying can be like knocking on God's door until He answers, just like I did.".......................

Corny Knock Knock Jokes!

"Knock Knock!"   "Who's there?"
"Jo"   "Jo who?"
"Jo - seph" HA HA!!
Joseph was Jesus Christ our Lord and Savior's step father!
(You can read about Joseph in the Books of Matthew and Luke).

My Special Prayer:

_____

_____

_____

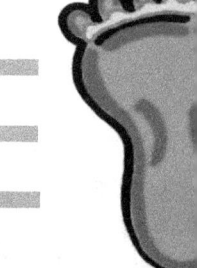

Rufus and Clyde and The Stench of Doom

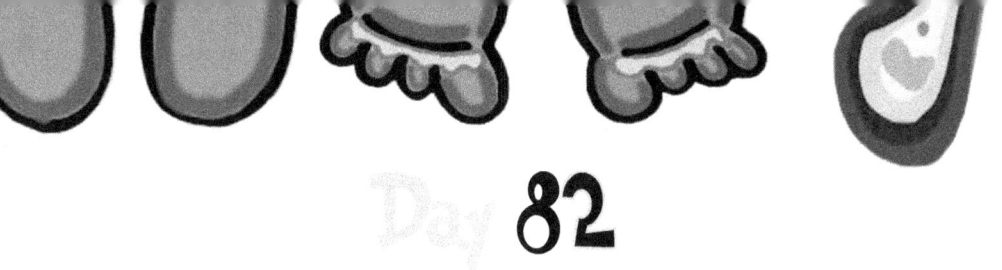

Day 82

READ (2 CHRONICLES 26:5) KJV

Corny Knock Knock Jokes!

"Knock Knock!"   "Who's there?"
"Com"   "Com who?"
"Com - forter" HA HA!!
The Holy Spirit is our comforter and guide to following Christ!
Amen!

This is a little bit of yesterday's story, see if you can read it Mirror style

............"That's not quite right you two. The asking part is like having a question for God, so you ask in prayer. Sort of like how you both questioned people in the house about the smell. The seeking part is the effort we put into getting our answers by searching and reading our bible. Like how both of you searched every room for that smell without giving up. And finally, praying can be like knocking on God's door until He answers, just like I did."..........

Hint: Place backward words above in front of a mirror and watch the words appear normal!

Pretty Good!!

Rufus and Clyde and The Stench of Doom

Play Cards!!

 Day 83

(Matthew 10:39) "He that findeth his life shall lose it: and he that loseth his life for my sake shall **find** it"

Corny Knock Knock Jokes!

"Knock Knock!"   "Who's there?"
"Mo"   "Mo who?"
"Mo - ses" HA HA!!

Moses was a mighty man of God who was used to help set the Israelites free from captivity.(You can read about his story in the book of Exodus).

HERE ARE SOME CLUES TO TOMORROW'S STORY:

So what do you think of the clues for tomorrow's story, think you can figure out what will happen?
Seek out some ideas while playing Memory Cards from Day 6!

1. Mix them up   2. Place them face down
3. Match all the cards that are alike

Incredible!!

Rufus and Clyde and The Stench of Doom

Day 4

..........They reached Rufus door. "I hope I shed some light on the true meaning of the scripture for you two. Rufus and Clyde just looked at each other a bit puzzled. It had been a long night for these two and they were both ready for bed. This scripture lesson proved to be a bit much and went over both of their heads. Mrs. Wyde could see that by the reaction on their faces.

"Oh never mind, we'll talk about it tomorrow after breakfast. You both get some sleep, goodnight"

"Goodnight mom"

"Goodnight Mrs. Wyde" They entered the room and closed the door.

Rufus looked at Clyde. "I don't get it". He scratched his head and yawned. "I'm going to sleep". He plopped on his bed and pulled the covers over him.

"All I know is this Rufus, the next sleep over we have will be at my house!"

Well, it looks like Mr. Wyde will be cleaning up his act!
Below is a list of stinky sins that we should ALL avoid.
Cross out the sins and circle the things that would please God.

Read (Luke 19:3) KJV

Reading the Bible	Being sneaky	Stealing
Praying	Listening	Being obedient
Lying to parents	Making fun of people	Making smart decisions
Being a friend	Sharing your faith	Getting into trouble
Helping at home	Frowning	Being polite
Cheating in school	Hurting people	Being honest
Not being obedient	Loving your neighbor	Being rude
Doing your homework	Smiling	Trusting God
Being nice to others	Being a bully	Being loving

Rufus and Clyde and The Stench of Doom

Yuck Yuck

Day 85

In Conclusion:
MR. WYDE WASHED HIS STINKY FEET!

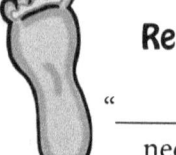

Read (2 Timothy 2: 15) KJV and fill in the missing words:

"_____to shew thyself_____unto God, a workman_____ needeth not to be ashamed,_____dividing the_____of truth"

Rufus and Clyde and The Stench of Doom

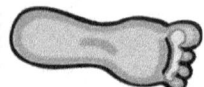

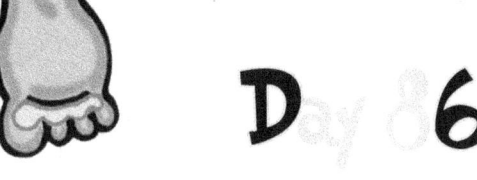

Day 86

Read (Proverbs 3:13) KJV

Corny Knock Knock Jokes!

"Knock Knock!"   "Who's there?"
"Pe"   "Pe who?"
"Pe—ter HA HA!!"
Peter was one of the twelve disciples of Jesus Christ in the New Testament! (You can read about his story in the books of Matthew, Mark, Luke and John just to name a few).

TRUE OR FALSE/YES OR NO

(Yes or No) It was Rufus and Clyde's stink bomb prank that stunk up the house?

A. Yes
B. No

(True or False) Rufus is over Clyde's house spending the night?

A. True
B. False

(True or False) Rufus and Clyde were dreaming of the stinky odor?

A. True
B. False

(True or False) Rufus and Clyde's stinky odor adventure happened at night-time?

A. True
B. False

You're the apple of God's eye!!

Rufus and Clyde and The Stench of Doom

Day 87

Read **(MATTHEW 7:14) KJV** and fill in the missing words:

"Because strait is the_____, and narrow is the way, which leadeth unto_____, and few there be that_____it"

Corny Knock Knock Jokes!

"Knock Knock!"   "Who's there?"
"Jo"   "Jo who?"
"Jo - nah" **HA HA!!**

Jonah was a prophet used by God in the Old Testament!
(You can read about his story in the book of Jonah).

Mrs. Wyde Fun Facts!

First Name:	Crystal
Last Name:	Wyde
Age:	39 years old
Address:	42 Sands Street in Manna's Ville
Hobbies:	Mrs. Wyde enjoys reading, spending time with friends, exercising, going to the salon and dancing.
Goals:	Getting people to eat her food! She believes she's a great cook and likes to experiment with different ingredient's to make food interesting!

Unbelievable!!

Rufus and Clyde and The Stench of Doom

HoneyKeep Ministries
HoneyKeep Ministries
HoneyKeep Minis
HoneyKeep Ministrie
HoneyKeep Minis
HoneyKeep Ministries

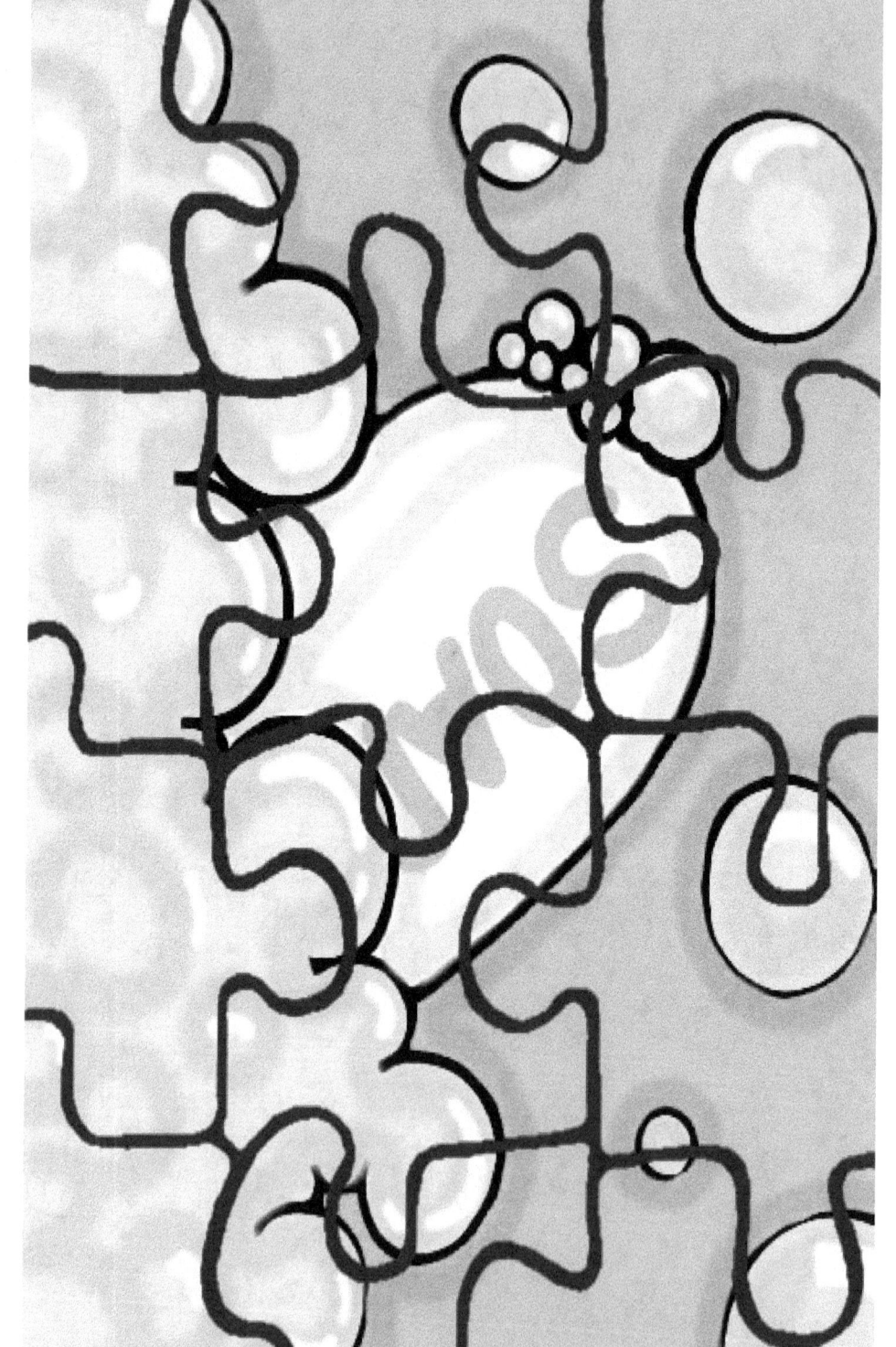

Day 88

Nice to Meet You!:

READ **(Psalm 24:6) KJV** AND FILL IN THE MISSING WORDS:

"This is_____generation of them that_____him, that
seek thy face, O_____. Selah"

CORNY KNOCK KNOCK JOKES!

"Knock Knock!"   "Who's there?"
"Han"   "Han who?"
"Han - nah" **HA HA!!**
Hannah was a women of God with great faith! She was blessed with
a miracle child named Samuel who became a mighty prophet!
(Her story can be found in the Old Testament book of 1 Samuel).

Your Fun Facts!

NOW IT'S TIME TO SHARE SOME FUN FACTS ABOUT YOURSELF BELOW:

First Name:	
Last Name:	
Age:	
Boy/Girl:	
Hobbies:	
Goals:	

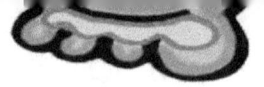

Draw-A-Doodle!!

Day 89

Read (Proverbs 8:35) KJV

Corny Knock Knock Jokes!

"Knock Knock!"   "Who's there?"
"No"   "No who?"
"No - ah" HA HA!!

Noah was a man of God who built an ark in the Old Testament!
(You can read about his story in the book of Genesis).

so creative!!

Can you draw this
picture of both
Rufus and Clyde
together?
Try it!

Rufus and Clyde and The Stench of Doom

Day 90

"Seeking God"
Read (MATTHEW 7: 7-8) KJV

Have you ever been excited about doing something or going somewhere? Just think about it. It feels good to receive an invite to a party, or better yet when people attend your own. How about going to a new movie you're really interested in seeing. Some of us are even excited about going to school, while others may be more excited in leaving to go home. Think about that thing that makes you the most happy. All of those positive feeling of excitement and joy are what God feels when we get on our knees, seek His face, read our bible and pray to Him. He enjoys hearing us knocking on His door, we are truly His guests of honor. Let's not keep Him waiting, pray and read your word today.

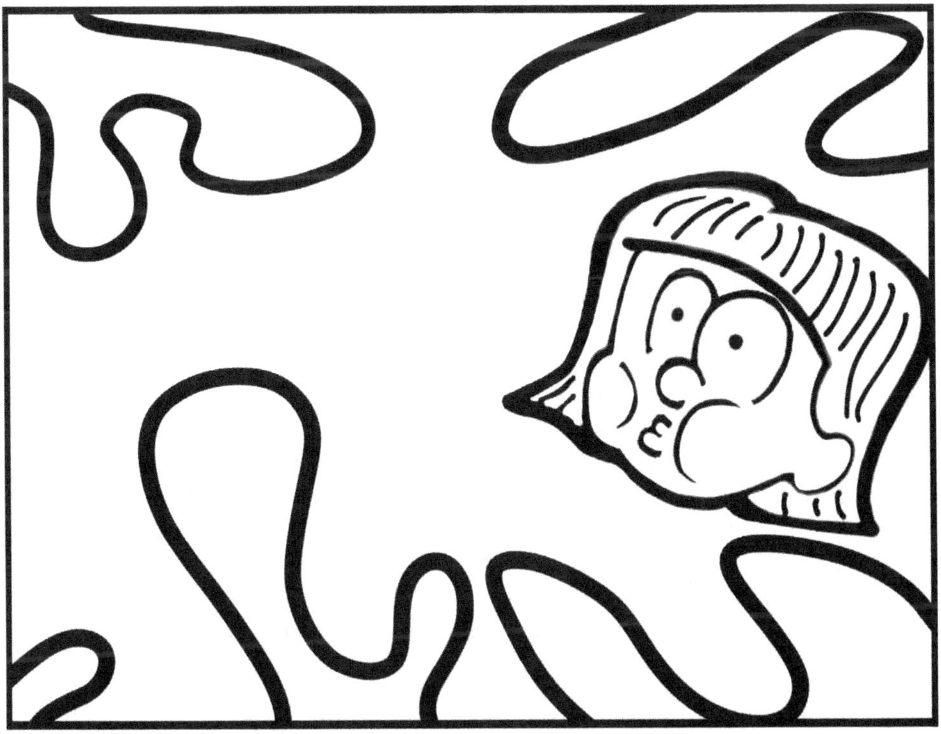

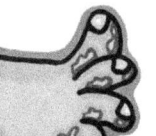

Rufus and Clyde and The Stench of Doom

"SHOW ME THE LIGHT"

WE ARE IN THE DARK, NOT KNOWING THAT WE'RE IN DARKNESS.

WE GO ABOUT OUR EVERYDAY LIVES IN TOTAL DARKNESS.

NOT KNOWING THAT THERE IS A BETTER WAY TO LIVE, TO FUNCTION OR EVEN TO EXIST.

BUT WAIT!
THERE IS A LIGHT AND A PERSON STANDING INSIDE THIS RADIANT LIGHT.

Continued . . . . .

SUDDENLY; THE WORLD LOOKS DIFFERENT INSIDE THIS LIGHT.

YOU LOOK AND SEE EVEN BETTER THAN BEFORE SINCE COMING INTO THE LIGHT.

I'M GOING TO CONTINUE TO WALK IN THE LIGHT, AMEN!

Salvation

IF YOU WANT TO BE SAVED (WHICH MEANS GIVING YOUR LIFE OVER TO CHRIST), YOU MUST REPEAT THIS SINNER'S PRAYER:

"Dear Lord, I am a sinner and I confess that Jesus Christ has died upon the cross and rose again for my sins, and that He is the Son of God. Please forgive me and be my Lord and Savior, Amen"

Please take the time to **find a church home** where you can grow and prosper within Christ. It is very important to be around people who are like minded. This is where your **strength** and **support** is, and this is the place where you can grow and learn more about God. **Don't give up or get discouraged** because hard times will come, it's something we all have to endure. Don't worry you will get wiser and stronger. Be blessed and keep the faith!

HoneyKeep Ministries ™

THANKS FOR ALLOWING US TO GROW IN GOD WITH YOU,
AND WE HOPE YOU ENJOYED THIS 90 DAY SILLY DEVOTIONAL!

THIS IS OUR FIRST CHILDREN'S BOOK PUBLISHED, AND WE HOPE
TO FURTHER THE KINGDOM WITH MORE INSPIRATIONAL BOOKS.
WE TAKE SPECIAL DELIGHT IN BRINGING SMILES TO CHILDREN
FACES AND WARMING THE HEART OF ADULTS WHO ARE TRUE
CHILDREN-AT-HEART!

PLEASE VISIT OUR WEBSITE AT :

www.honeykeepministries.org

AND FOLLOW US ON

TWITTER @hkmbooks AND

FACEBOOK @honeykeepministries

TO HEAR ABOUT OUR LATEST NEWS AND RECENTLY PUBLISHED
MATERIALS. BE BLESSED AND KEEP READING!

Get the

HoneyKeep Ministries

eyKeep Ministries

HoneyKeep Ministries

neyKeep Ministries

HoneyKeep Ministries

eyKeep Ministries

Answer Sheet

R	O	T	T	E	N							
											S	
		M	A	T	T	H	E	W			M	
								S		E		
F	A	R	T		B				O		L	
				I				U		L		
E		J	O	B		B		R		Y		
X				Y		L			M			
O			K			E	L				J	
D			N			A				O		
U		U			S				E			
S	K			P				L				
	S	C	O	R	N	C	H	I	P	S		

DAY 8

1. What food was Rufus and Clyde dreaming about?
   - **a. Tacos**
   - b. cheese burgers
   - c. candy
   - d. pizza

2. Name three things the odor smelled like?
   - a. hairspray, coffee, grass
   - b. perfume, candles, in-scents
   - **c. gym socks, farts, skunks**
   - d. spoiled milk, onions, garlic

3. What was Rufus and Clyde doing?
   - a. playing video games
   - **b. sleeping**
   - c. watching t.v.
   - d. playing outside

4. Who did Rufus and Clyde blame the smell on?
   - a. a neighbor
   - b. a ghost
   - c. a pet
   - **d. each other**

DAY 10

First Row:
Wonderful
Counselor
Prince of Peace
Yahweh
Savior

Second Row:
Christ
Alpha
I Am
Omega
Father

Third Row:
High Priest
Shepard
Carpenter
Jesus
Abba

DAY 14

Who's idea was it to search outside the room?
A. Clyde
B. Rufus
C. Mr. Wyde (Rufus Dad)
D. Mrs. Wyde (Rufus Mom)

What did Rufus and Clyde find when searching for the smell?
A. Sunglasses, hats and gloves
B. Used tooth brush, tissue and paper
C. Dirty socks, under garments and used gum
D. Chips, broccoli and spinach

Where was some places Rufus and Clyde looked for the smell?
A. Behind the T.V. and under a blanket
B. In the laundry basket and in a box
C. In the kitchen and in the bathroom
D. Under the bed and in the closet.

What did Rufus and Clyde turn on to search for the odor?
A. A flashlight
B. The light switch
C. The T.V.
D. The cell phone

DAY 19

Church - House of God

Shepard - Preacher

Praise - Worship

Fruit of the Spirit - Love, Joy, Peace

God's Word - Bible

DAY 20

What room was Rufus and Clyde in?
A. Living Room   B. Basement   C. Kitchen   D. Bedroom

The Chicken Pot Pie Casserole had what inside of it?
A. Feathers   B. Chicken   C. Rice   D. Legs

The Buttered Biscuits were like what?
A. Fluffy Soft   B. Hard as a Rock   C. Lightly toasted   D. Moldy Green

What desert did Rufus and Clyde find Upside Down?
A. The Apple Pie   B. The Jell-O   C. The Rice Pudding   D. The Cake

Who was Rufus and Clyde talking to in the kitchen?
A. Rufus Cousin   **B. Rufus Mom**   C. Rufus Sister
D. Rufus Grandpa

What was the scripture Mrs. Wyde used for the game?
A. Brotherly Love   B. Armor of God   C. The Beattitudes
D. Ask, Seek & Knock

What did Rufus & Clyde think the scripture meant?
A. Knock Knock Jokes B. Wisdom   C. don't be bad
D. Be a Nice person

							M	O	S	E	S
	S	T	I	N	K						
J				A		G	H	A	S	T	L
O					B						
S					R		N	O	A	H	
E	J	E	S	U	S		A				
P							H				
H								A			G
	M	I	L	D	E	W			M		A
O							Y				S
	D					R					
		O				A		F	O	U	L
		R		M							

First Row:

Peace
Protector
Teacher
Strength

Second Row:

Friend
Happiness
Joy
Healer

Third Row:

Good Listener
Kindness
Father
Love

DAY 37

What question did Grandpa Morris ask Rufus and Clyde when he seen them?

A. "Are you having an adventure?"
B. "Do you both need to use the bathroom?"
C. "What time is it?"
D. "Can you help me back to my room?"

What sound did Rufus and Clyde hear when they were looking for Grandpa Morris?

A. Music & singing
B. Toilet flushing & running water
C. Shower running
D. Brushing teeth

Who was responsible for the new odor Rufus and Clyde began to smell?

A. Rufus   B. Clyde
C. Mrs Wyde   **D. Grandpa Morris**

What does Grandpa Morris use to help him walk better?

A. A walker   B. A wheelchair
C. A cane   D. A crutch

DAY 39

Noah - Ark
Whale - Jonah
Baby Jesus - Manger
Salvation - Cross
Moses - Ten Commandments

DAY 42

Adam - Genesis
John the Baptist - Matthew
Judges - Samson
Giant Goliath - 1 Samuel
1 Kings - Solomon

DAY 43

What is the baby's name mentioned by Grandpa Morris?

A. Jesse   B. John
C. James   D. Little J.

What is the baby's mother name mentioned by Grandpa Morris?

A. Theresa   **B. Tonya**
C. Tiffany   D. Tara

Why did Grandpa Morris blame the baby?

A. Because his diapers were very smelly
B. Because he cried all day
C. Because the baby told him
D. Because the baby made a mess

Grandpa Morris went where after talking with Rufus & Clyde?

A. To the kitchen to get a snack
B. To the living room to watch T.V.
C. He left the house and went home
D. Back to his room

First Row:
Friend
Deliverer
Healer
Miracle
Worker

Second Row:
Listener
Provider
Comforter

Third Row:
Savior
Father
Teacher
Protector

What was Tonya and baby James doing when Rufus and Clyde came into their room?

A. They were sleeping
B. Tonya was reading to Baby James
C. They were playing
D. Watching T.V.

How is Tonya related to Rufus?

A. She's his mother
B. She's his best friend
C. She's his neighbor
D. She's his cousin

Why did Rufus and Clyde want to talk to Tonya?

A. They wanted to say goodnight
B. They wanted to play a prank
C. She might be the cause of the bad smell
D. She asked them to come

What was Tonya holding in her hands?

A. Tissue
B. T.V. remote control
C. A soiled diaper
D. Nothing

I	S	A	I	A	H							B
						P				O		
H	E	B	R	E	W	S		S		J		A
								A				C
J	O	H	N			S				L		T
				I						M	S	
			S		J	U	D	E				
		E		E						T		
	N			S					I			
	E			T				T				
G		J	O	N	A	H		H			U	
							E		S			
	R	O	M	A	N	S		R				

What was the waste basket full of in Tonya and baby James room?

A. Spoiled food
B. Dirty laundry
C. Smelly diapers
D. Perfume

What size was the waste basket in Tonya and Baby James room?

A. Hugh
B. Small
C. Large
D. Medium

Rufus and Clyde noticed what returning back in the hallway?

A. T.V. in the living room was on
B. Everyone was asleep
C. The smell was gone
D. The odor was still there

Who did Rufus and Clyde think was right about Tonya and baby James causing the stink?

A. Grandpa Morris
B. Mr. Wyde
C. Mrs.Wyde
D. Aliens from space

DAY 66

P		M	E	E	K	N	E	S	S	L		G	
	E								O		N		
		A					R		I				P
L		C			T		R			K			A
O			E		N		E			I			T
U				O		F		J		N			I
E			C		F			O		D			E
		F		U				Y		N			N
	L		S							E			C
	E	G		F	R	U	I	T		S			E
S		N								S			
	O		G	E	N	T	L	E	N	E	S	S	
L													

DAY 67

What was Rufus and Clyde doing with Mr. Wyde?

A. Eating and watching a movie
B. Playing video games
C. Talkng about school and grades
D. Helping clean up

What did Rufus and Clyde almost forget about?

A. What they ate for dinner
B. Going to bed
C. Talking to Tonya
D. The stinky odor

(True or False) Was this sentence in yesterday's story: "They were having too much fun!"

A. True
B. False

(Yes or No) Was this sentence in yesterday's story: "They made the problem bigger by focusing on it"

A. Yes
B. No

DAY 69

First Row:
Jude
Titus
Ruth

Second Row:
St. John
Micah
Esther

Third Row:
Jonah
Amos
Luke

DAY 73

What did Rufus and Clyde discover?

A. Dirty socks
B. Hidden candy
C. Mr. Wyde's smelly feet
D. More of Baby James diapers

(True or False) "Mrs. Wyde food was the cause of the horrible smell!"

A. True   B. False

Who did Rufus think about to tell his father about his feet?

A. His mom   B. Grandpa Morris
C. Tonya   D. His friend Clyde

(Yes or No) Was this sentence in yesterday's story: "We'll get my mom to do it for us"

A. Yes   B. No

DAY 75

Jesus Christ - Died on the Cross
Sarai - Gave birth at old age
Jonah - Swallowed by whale
Mary - Gave birth to Jesus
John the Baptist - Baptized Jesus in water

DAY 79

Where did Mrs. Wyde walk the boys to get some sleep?

A. To Clyde's house
B. Rufus bedroom
C. The tree house
D. To Baby James crib

(True or False) Mrs. Wyde has tried to get Mr. Wyde to throw away his shoes!"

A. True
B. False

(Yes or No) Was this sentence in yesterday's story:
"They were relieved."

A. Yes
B. No

(True or False) Mrs. Wyde assured the boys that she would take care of the problem."

A. True
B. False

DAY 84

First Row:

Cross Out:
Lying to parents
Cheating in school
Not being obedient

Circle:
Reading the Bible
Praying
Being a friend
Helping at home
Doing your homework
Being nice to others

Second Row:

Cross Out:
Being sneaky
Making fun of people
Frowning
Hurting people
Being a bully

Circle:
Listening
Sharing your faith
Loving your neighbor
Smiling

Third Row:

Cross Out:
Stealing
Getting into trouble
Being rude

Circle:
Being obedient
Making smart decisions
Being polite
Being honest
Trusting God
Being loving

DAY 86

(Yes or No) It was Rufus and Clyde's stink bomb prank that stunk up the house?

A. Yes
B. No

(True or False) Rufus is over Clyde's house spending the night?

A. True
B. False

(True or False) Rufus and Clyde were dreaming of the stinky odor?

A. True
B. False

(True or False) Rufus and Clyde's stinky odor adventure happened at night-time?

A. True
B. False